Ganymede's Cup

A Novel

Beverly R. Sherringham

iUniverse, Inc.

New York   Bloomington

iUniverse books may be ordered through booksellers or by contacting:

iUniverse
1663 Liberty Drive
Bloomington, IN 47403
www.iuniverse.com
1-800-Authors (1-800-288-4677)

Because of the dynamic nature of the Internet, any Web addresses or links
contained in this book may have changed since publication and may no longer be
valid. The views expressed in this work are solely those of the author and do not
necessarily reflect the views of the publisher, and the publisher hereby disclaims
any responsibility for them.

ISBN: 978-1-4502-6981-0 (sc)
ISBN: 978-1-4502-6982-7 (ebook)

Printed in the United States of America

iUniverse rev. date: 11/09/2010

To Mrs. Alfred Gellhorn

Words of encouragement can inspire a life. Thank you.

Beginnings

The fish were biting, and the grandfather patiently directed his grandson's attention to the pond, in which tiny bubbles indicated that a fish was approaching the young man's line.

"Winston," whispered his grandfather, "turn around and look at your line. I think you've got one."

The young man continued to look upward towards the spires of the high school. Yes, he was certain. He saw a picture of an eagle in his kindergarten class. It was an eagle all right.

"Grandpa, there's an eagle up there," said the young man pointing towards the spires.

"Shh!" admonished the grandfather. "Do you want to scare the fish away? Turn around and look down at the water. Don't you see those bubbles? You're going to get a fish."

The young man's gaze continued to look upward at the eagle perched atop the spires. It was regal, majestic, and imperious. Without a sound, it lifted its wings and flew towards the heavens.

"Grandpa, look!" said the young man pointing towards the sky. "There he goes!"

"Now look what you did," said the grandfather with annoyance. "You scared the fish away."

The grandfather packed the fishing gear. "Come on, we may as well go home."

"Sorry, Grandpa," said the young man sorrowfully.

"Boy, there aren't any eagles in these parts. You have to go out West to see an eagle.

What would an eagle be doing here in New Jersey? It was probably a crow or something. You scared the fish away, Winston. Let's go home to your grandmother. I'll never make a fisherman out of you."

The young man picked up his fishing rod and followed his grandfather while looking up at the spires. "It *was* an eagle," whispered the boy to himself.

Prelude

Sheridon Southgate's image graces the cover of the May issue of *Business Week*. Although he is beginning to manifest signs of premature baldness, Sheridon's striking image commands respect from business leaders around the world and adoration from a plethora of beauties of all ages and nationalities. Takeovers are Sheridon's specialty. Sheridon's wealth and stature are boresome; the attainment of money and prestige are no longer viable incentives. If the truth be told, Sheridon Southgate can find little reason to endure another day of tedious takeovers and heart-wrenching deconstruction of others' lives and dreams. The doorbell chimes in the wee small hours of the fashionable section of London. Unable to sleep, Sheridon welcomes the intrusion to the overwhelming silence and walks sluggishly to the door of his modest townhome. A small picnic basket nestles unobtrusively amidst the fragrant, flowering blooms cascading over the sides of an oblong, wooden planter on the step. Traces of heavy perfume compete with the gentle aroma of the cheerful flowers in the crisp, dark air. Sheridon recognizes Nicole's perfume.

Nicole is a moody French artist, with whom Sheridon has a brief dalliance in the cool, refined London summer. At the onset of winter, Nicole vanishes almost as abruptly as she enters Sheridon's tumultuous life. The picnic basket is *par for the course*. It is only fitting that Nicole returns with a peace offering, especially one ensconced within the picnic basket they shared on their first picnic near the Italian fountains in Hyde Park. Sheridon recalls Nicole's prowess in the kitchen and the morsels she prepares to whet his finicky palette. A lover of games, Sheridon decides to play and retrieves the basket from the planter. Gingerly, he places the basket upon the soft, white sofa. Sheridon opens the drapes to watch for Nicole's advance and envisions her outfit. A style maven, Nicole wears surprisingly understated clothing. Sheridon hopes that the green, flowered chiffon affair that he remembers from their first picnic will adorn her thin, elegant body. The sheer, flowing dress clung to her petite frame; Sheridon mischievously remembers wishing for rain. After a few moments, the wistful, anticipatory smile disappears from his eager face. Anxiously, Sheridon opens the door and looks around; no one is there.

Dear Reader, must you be told the outcome? Have you not read enough novels with similar themes to anticipate what will transpire? Yes, Sheridon opens the basket and finds a tiny infant wrapped in a red and white checkered tablecloth, the same tablecloth from his first picnic with Nicole. The cheerful, blue-eyed infant with the *café au lait* complexion rests comfortably next to an expensive claret and a generous portion of Edam cheese—Sheridon's favorites. An engraved, buff invita Business Week tion card with gold calligraphic lettering tucked inside of the infant's royal blue sleepwear introduces Sheridon to his son. A postscript written in Nicole's hand announces, "Your son is named Guy (pronounced Ghee). I tell you this, Sheridon, for I fear your vulgar American enunciation." The note is succinct. Sheridon turns the card over, but there are no other words. Sheridon observes the silent infant as he pours the claret into an elegant crystal flute. The delectable wine and savory cheese bring a smile to Sheridon's appreciative lips. Nicole's impeccable taste and generosity do not disappoint.

Sheridon carries the basket into the bedroom and places it on the rumpled bed while eyeing its contents curiously. He packs a small bag and books passage on British Airways' first flight from Heathrow to JFK. For the first time in six years, Sheridon visits his widowed father's modest suburban home in northern New Jersey. The grandfather stands agog as his son deposits Guy, the picnic basket, and a generous check on the dining room table. Sheridon Southgate returns to London before sunrise on British Airways' first flight from JFK to Heathrow to put the finishing touches on a strategic takeover (his twenty-second) of a paper manufacturing company. Lamentably, the new grandfather, Winston Churchill Brielle, has nothing to cushion the shock of the unsettling appearance of an infant grandson enveloped in a strange aroma of wine and cheese, nestled in a picnic basket, and wrapped in a red-checkered tablecloth.

Chapter I

Sunbeams glitter on the pond as students cross the bridge enroute to morning classes at the high school. The gentle sound of water cascades over the rocks of a diminutive but respectable waterfall. The scenic beauty is taken for granted, for it has become a part of the daily routine. The spires atop the high school tower bespeak classical elegance, though no one casts a glance upward to pay tribute. Seated upon a red, plaid blanket is a gentleman with distinguished graying temples and warm, brown eyes, which are closed as he rests his head against a large elm tree near the bank of the pond. Ducks glide slowly across the gelatin surface of the shimmering waters. The sound of the miniature waterfall is therapeutic. Visions of a petite, youthful teenager with short, brown curls bring a smile to the gentleman's lips. The smell of honeysuckle magically fills his senses, as it is wont to do whenever he thinks of Chloe. Chloe's image is timeless. The long-limbed widower tries to imagine his deceased wife as a middle-aged woman, but he cannot. Chloe was nineteen years of age when she died giving birth to their only child. Her happy, youthful face is the only image Winston can evoke.

"Are you sleeping, Grandpa?"

A young boy stands on the bank holding a small fishing rod into the pond. Winston Churchill Brielle opens his eyes, and the smell of honeysuckle and Chloe's image dissipate.

"No, Guy, I'm just resting my eyes."

Guy laughs. "You always say that, Grandpa, then you fall asleep in your chair."

"Grandpa needs his rest to keep up with you, Guy. I think that we can go home now. The fish don't seem to be biting this morning."

"I want to stay and catch a fish. I see one right there." Guy pointed into the pond where tiny bubbles scratched the surface.

"All right. We'll stay five more minutes, and then we'll go and have a few pancakes at IHOP."

Guy's enthusiastic response brings a smile to his grandfather's face but frightens the fish away. Guy places his rod on the blanket.

"Let's go now, Grandpa. I want strawberry waffles with cream on top."

Guy's face shines like a sunbeam, and his brown, curly hair moves restlessly with each of his movements. Guy is tall for his age and possesses a rather ironic gaze at times that juxtaposes cryptic determination with an innocent vulnerability. Reader, oftentimes, one never knows whether to hug Guy with open arms or with an armored vest. At times, Guy resembles his other grandfather, Herman Southgate, who opposed the marriage of his precious daughter, Chloe, to the son of a widow living on a pension in a working class section of northern New Jersey. It did not matter that Winston and Chloe were university classmates. Lineage was everything to the erudite Herman Southgate, descendant of a long line of prosperous, Cleveland dentists, and he feared that his grandchildren would be a rather coarse lot with the infusion of Brielle blood, the blood of common laborers. Herman Southgate attempted to browbeat his devastated son-in-law into relinquishing his newborn son when Chloe died, but his attempts were unsuccessful. Lamentably, after a year of negotiating the cost of completing his education, caring for his mother, who suffered a near-fatal stroke, and discovering that he had a heart mummer that depleted his strength at indiscriminate times, Winston filled an old leather satchel with his infant son's favorite toys and meager belongings and boarded a train to Cleveland, Ohio to relinquish his son, Anthony Brielle, named after his deceased paternal grandfather, to the vibrant maternal grandfather, Herman Southgate, who immediately renamed the infant Sheridon Southgate, after the first Southgate to attain a degree in dentistry.

Winston ambled slowly behind Guy as the vivacious youth skipped gaily over the diminutive bridge. Winston anticipated a restful morning ensconced within the supple leather of his brown wing chair while smoking his pipe, sipping his port wine, and reading his mysteries. Sick leave had its benefits. The old heart beat merrily within the confines of Winston's den but raced fiercely within his pressure-filled principal's office. The angst-ridden adolescents would have to inflict their terror upon some other altruistic soul. Thoughts of retirement loomed large, and the thoughts were ever so pleasing.

Chapter II

The jazz band set up the stage in the World Trade Center Plaza. People began to fill the chairs that were strategically placed behind the spouting fountain. An upbeat tune filled the air with festivity. Arnold Cohen leaned his head back and closed his eyes behind his sunglasses. All external thoughts were assuaged by the glistening sun, which messaged his face and forehead.

"Mr. Cohen?" Arnold frowned as a quiet, figure blocked the sun.

"How did you find me, Lawrence? Don't you have enough work to do?"

"I'm sorry to disturb you, Sir, but these papers are in need of your signature."

The youthful intern stood before the aging CEO in a crisp, blue and white pinstriped, long-sleeved shirt with buttoned neck and cuffs flavored with a pale blue tie, unseasonable gray slacks, and brown oxford shoes. Arnold removed his sunglasses and sat upright. The remnants of his red, curly hair intermingled with the gray strands that were taking over his hairline.

"Do you like jazz, Lawrence?"

"Not really, Sir," confessed Lawrence.

"Then give me the papers and go back inside. You're blocking the sun."

"Yes, Sir." Lawrence gathered the papers after they had been signed and disappeared into the North Tower. The jazz trio featured a soloist, who began the lunchtime concert with a melancholy song accompanied by a trumpet. Arnold closed his eyes again as the singer's voice emitted a soothing balm of smooth jazz.

On the eighty-first floor of the North Tower. Daniel Cohen waited anxiously for the return of the signed papers. "Did he sign them?" asked Daniel anxiously.

"Yes, Sir," answered Lawrence placing the treasures into his employer's hands.

"Next week this time, Lawrence, I will be the happiest man on earth." Daniel placed the folder on his uncluttered, organized desk. "Where do you live, Lawrence?"

"I have a room near the university, Sir."

"What would you say if I told you that my new house on the North Shore of Long Island has fourteen rooms?" asked Daniel proudly.

"I'd say that you were quite fortunate, Sir."

"Do you know why I am fortunate, Lawrence?"

The obvious answer was that Daniel Cohen's family was old money, but the youth remained silent as his employer continued. "I make wise decisions, Lawrence, and I am not afraid to take risks. Hiring you as an intern was the wisest decision I made this year. You are invaluable to this firm, Lawrence. Did you know that?"

"Thank you, Sir," said Lawrence sheepishly.

"Lawrence, I would like to invite you to a family gathering next week in honor of my daughter's graduation from high school."

"Next week, Sir? I think that I may have a final next week."

"I haven't told you the day," persisted Daniel.

"I meant that I am studying for finals next week, Sir."

"I am going to insist that you take a break and attend this gathering. Networking is crucial if you intend to make it in this business. Gangly, squealing girls in braces will flounce around in gowns they haven't the figures to fill yet, but their fathers and grandfathers, heads of the most prestigious firms in the city, will also be in attendance. You wouldn't want to miss this opportunity, Lawrence, would you?" Daniel reached for the photo of his daughter on the desk and placed it before the intern.

"She's quite lovely, Sir."

"Lovely? Sara is beautiful, Lawrence."

Stephen's eyes were drawn to the brooding figure in a tuxedo seated behind a cello on the other side of the double frame.

"That's my son, Jonathan. He's finishing grad school in New Haven. Jonathan has a chamber music group. Do you like chamber music, Lawrence?"

"Another music question," thought the intern impatiently. He smiled and answered, "Not really, Sir, but I'm certain that your son's group is exemplary. Will they be performing at the affair?" asked Lawrence cautiously. Networking with top executives was one thing, but expecting him to sit through an evening of chamber music was an excruciating thought.

Daniel chuckled and placed the picture on the desk. "No, I'm afraid we will have to sit through the trendy music of the young, Lawrence. Are you willing to brave it?"

"It will be my pleasure, Sir," said the intern trying to divert his gaze away from the self-absorbed cellist in the photo.

Chapter III

The band played a soft, bouncy tune. Although the young people pretended to enjoy the rhythms, most were accustomed to music with less bounce and more throb. Arnold Cohen swirled his wife, Susannah, around the glossy ballroom floor. Susannah, a pediatrician, wore a long, green dress off the rack at a discount department store. After years of struggling through medical school after a failed marriage to a disabled Vietnam veteran, Susannah retained the characteristics of a simple woman with a desire to serve the less fortunate. Her acorn brown ponytail danced to its own rhythm and made her look exceedingly youthful. Around her limp, brown eyes she carried the travail of a mother, who left her young son with a mentally unstable father in order to pursue her dream of becoming a doctor. Arnold, her husband of thirty years, made the journey palatable. Without Arnold, she would not have accomplished her dream; instead, she would have been ensconced within a tiny, cheerless apartment in San Francisco nursing a man eaten alive with bitterness and grief. That was the past.

The present was much more cheerful. The ballrooom, decorated with brilliant floral bouquets, happy balloons, and flouncy ribbons, was rather juvenile for the tastes of the young adults preparing to leave the cocooned world of high school, but they endured quietly anticipating the extravagant gifts that they were destined to attain as they embarked upon the educational paths of sororities, fraternities, and, perhaps, a few engaging courses that would prepare them for their stations in life.

The tables were adorned with white linen tablecloths, elegant, crystal candelabras, and bouquets of shimmering white floral arrangements. The intern, sitting alone in a far corner towards the back of the room, noted that the table settings were more suited for the adults than for the young graduates. From his rear seat, the intern observed some of the youthful guests as they made their way around the tables cagily sipping champagne from unattended glasses. One clever young lady managed to obtain an entire bottle of champagne. In a darkened corner outside of the ballroom, several students took swigs from the bottle and giggled merrily. The remainder of the champagne was poured into glasses of punch. The students dispersed and entered the ballroom with a bit more bounce in their steps and laughter in their voices. The young lady placed the empty bottle on the intern's empty table, winked mischievously, and joined her friends on the dance floor.

Elizabeth Cohen nudged her husband as they danced solemnly to the festive music. Her dress was a muted brown Oscar de la Renta original of classic elegance, and her raven hair was upswept and memorable. Elizabeth's generous heart was often overshadowed by her desire to wear the finest and to be seen with the most genteel people in the metropolitan area. As a youth, Elizabeth's dream was to grace the cover of *Vogue* magazine, but she was aware that someone of her background and breeding would not submit to having her image emblazoned on the cover of a fashion magazine like a common actress or model. Elizabeth settled for marriage with the son of a mogul, who would someday inherit the corporation, which might pay for the palatial fourteen-room house on the North Shore of Long Island that would soon be theirs.

"Who is that young man in the corner, Daniel? I don't believe that I have ever seen him before," remarked Elizabeth.

"That's Lawrence, my intern. I expect great things from him."

"You never mentioned that you had an intern. Look at him over there all alone."

"I'm going to introduce him to a few people. He's brilliant and has tremendous possibilities," responded Daniel eyeing one of the jolly students sneaking another sip from an unattended glass of champagne at an empty table. Daniel averted his eyes.

"Don't tell me that you're thinking of introducing him to Sara. You know how she hates it when you try to arrange meetings with young men you've selected for her."

"There's nothing wrong with an introduction or two. Lawrence is level-headed, ambitious, and a young man of character. It wouldn't hurt Sara to meet some new friends."

"What do you know about him? Who are his people?"

Daniel stopped dancing. "Let's sit for awhile, shall we?" Daniel led his wife to their table and asked a waiter to summon the intern to his table. The intern tried to shield his annoyance. In truth, he enjoyed observing the titans and their offspring away from the battleground of the financial capital of the world. He approached the table cheerfully.

"Lawrence, this is my wife, Elizabeth."

"Pleased to make your acquaintance," uttered Lawrence extending his hand.

"Sit beside me, Lawrence," said Elizabeth. "I would like to know more about you."

"Come with me, Lawrence," summoned Daniel. "I'd like to introduce you to a few people."

The intern followed Daniel around the room to make the acquaintance of some of the most powerful men in the business world. It gratified his heart that the moguls scheduled time to support the rite of passage of a colleague's daughter. Undoubtedly, their presence was predicated upon pending mergers or other financial concerns. Business worked hand-in-hand with pleasure and formed a formidable bond of common interests. Lawrence wondered if his handshake was firm enough and worried that his jacket was creased from the train ride to New Jersey. The fact that the intern did not wear a tuxedo endeared him within the hearts of the executives; he was bright, filled with solid integrity, and a fiscal virgin. One could mold a poor, hardworking student to meet the necessary corporate image. The intern was confident that he had made a good impression when he returned to his seat. The guest of honor was now seated beside him. Lawrence recognized her as the young woman guzzling the bottle of champagne. Sara smiled at him and was confident that he would not betray her.

"Lawrence, this is my daughter, Sara," said Daniel proudly.

Although Sara's carnation pink gown made her appear young and vulnerable, there was a gleam in her brown eyes that suggested that she was neither young nor vulnerable. The ingénue extended her delicate hand.

"I'm pleased to make your acquaintance, Lawrence," said Sara sweetly.

"Stephen," corrected the intern. "My name is Stephen Lawrence."

"Two first names—how clever." Sara turned to Arnold, who was standing and clinking a glass with a spoon.

"Here! Here! I would like to propose a toast." Arnold raised his glass. "I commend all of the graduates on their accomplishments. Many of you will be leaving to attend the finest universities in our great country."

"Please, make it brief, Arnold," whispered Susannah sensing the impatience of the youth.

"I know that you will make us very proud in the years to come. I think it only fitting that we support and encourage our youth."

As Arnold spoke, a tall, slender young man impeccably dressed in a black tuxedo with silk lapels entered the ballroom. Observing the speech in progress, he sat at a table in the back of the room. The young girls whispered amongst themselves and smiled in his direction. Jonathan Cohen was accustomed to creating a stir when he entered a room. The suave young man focused his attention upon the speaker. Even at a distance, his long, curly eyelashes graced his bluish gray eyes and enveloped him within an ethereal aura.

"I see that my grandson has arrived," said Arnold interrupting his toast. "Come up here, Jonathan, and join your family."

All eyes were on Jonathan as he walked with assured gracefulness towards the front of the room. Jonathan kissed his mother and sister while his peripheral vision surveyed the entire room. He was pleased that all eyes were still mesmerized by his presence.

"In that vein," Arnold continued, "I would like to present my granddaughter with her graduation present." Arnold produced an envelope with a picture of a giraffe, an elephant, and a group of jovial teenagers on safari.

"Grandfather, you didn't!" squealed Sara with excitement. The eager teen grasped the envelope from her grandfather's hand and opened it hastily. Her friends gathered around her.

"There's a car waiting for you outside that will take you to the airport. Your plane leaves at ten. If you leave now, you'll have plenty of time to meet the others. Your grandmother packed a small bag for you."

"What are you doing, Arnold?" asked Elizabeth nervously. Sara's graduation is tomorrow. She can't leave to go on a safari. We've already made plans for Sara to travel through Europe this summer." The anguished wife looked towards her husband in the hushed room. "Daniel, say something," demanded Elizabeth.

"Don't make a scene, Elizabeth. We can discuss this later," whispered Daniel.

"How can you just sit there? Say something!" screeched Elizabeth.

"Very well," said Daniel lifting his glass, "here's to a happy voyage!"

Sara squealed again and kissed her parents and grandparents. She hastened to the waiting limousine in the midst of a throng of ebullient, youthful well-wishers. A crestfallen Elizabeth walked swiftly to the ladies room. The music began again, and the festivities resumed. Susannah followed Elizabeth to the ladies room to offer solace.

"You might have consulted us first," chided Daniel.

Arnold smiled and raised his glass of champagne to his lips. "I will see you in my office tomorrow morning promptly at nine, Daniel. We can discuss the computer company you acquired in Nice, France without my authorization. I do believe that Nice was one of Sara's destinations on the proposed European jaunt you and your wife were planning to surprise her with. Mixing a little business with pleasure is to be commended, Daniel, but overstepping my authority is quite another matter. Daniel averted his eyes to the floor. Stephen looked from one Cohen to the other. Stephen researched the company in Nice and prepared most of the paperwork for the acquisition, but he had no idea that his astoundingly proficient work was unauthorized and hoped that he would not be culpable of any wrongdoing.

"I don't believe we've met," said Jonathan moving into his sister's vacant seat. "I'm Jonathan Cohen, son and grandson of the two combatants."

"Jonathan, this is Lawrence, a very bright intern your father hired. Perhaps a little too bright," said Arnold savoring the prime ribs and asparagus on his plate. "Pass the salt, please, Lawrence."

Stephen passed the salt in the gentle, crystal container with ornate gold top to his employer with a nervous hand.

"Lawrence is it?" asked Jonathan taking the salt from Stephen's trembling hand and passing it to his grandfather.

"Stephen Lawrence, actually," said Stephen nervously.

"Precisely what do you do in the firm, Stephen Lawrence?"

"Lawrence provides the brains for your father's clandestine activities, isn't that right, Lawrence?"

Stephen sat silent unsure of what to say. He looked at Daniel, but his employer's eyes were still downcast. Elizabeth and Susannah returned to the table.

"I'm going home," said Elizabeth softly. Her face was altered, and her eyes were weary with the tears of the hopeless. "I can't believe I won't get to see my own daughter graduate," she lamented. Daniel stood beside his wife. His eyes met neither his wife's nor his father's.

"You might have asked us first," said the cowering executive as he led his distraught wife to the door.

"I'll try to smooth things out," said Susannah as she followed her son and daughter-in-law.

Arnold wiped his mouth with his white, linen napkin and placed it back upon his lap.

"I'd better be going," said Stephen anxiously. "Thank you, Mr. Cohen, for the invitation. I enjoyed the evening."

"Not so fast, Lawrence, I want to see you in my office at nine along with your compatriot. Don't be late and bring all of the facts and figures you so amply supplied for that acquisition in Nice. You'd better bring your travel vouchers as well. I understand that you made three trips to Nice finalizing the deal. I hope that you enjoyed the trips; they will be your last."

"Sir, if I can just say…"

"Save it for the meeting tomorrow, Lawrence," said Arnold gruffly. "I think I'll have more of those prime ribs." Arnold summoned the waiter. Jonathan touched his grandfather's shoulder.

"I'll see Stephen out, Grandfather. I'm certain that he had no idea the Cohen torpedoes would be hurled in his direction when he accepted the invitation to this soiree."

Arnold continued to eat and moved his head cheerfully to the jubilant tune the band played. "Don't be too long, Jonathan. I want to hear all about your concert tour with that infernal chamber music group. I don't know why you didn't stick with the saxophone I bought you in sixth grade."

Jonathan smiled. "Grandfather, you are a treasure."

"I apologize for my grandfather's brusque manner," said Jonathan as he walked Stephen to the door. "I'd like to say that my family is not usually like this, but working closely with them, you must realize that they are not without their foibles."

Stephen's thoughts returned to Sara imbibing the champagne from the bottle, Daniel's fainthearted response to his father, and Arnold's questionable timing in presenting his granddaughter with a gift that would preclude her graduation.

"I'd just like to get the train back to the city," lamented Stephen.

Jonathan laughed. "Trains and buses are virtually nonexistent after rush hour in this area. Unless you're prepared to take a taxi back to New York, and judging from the salary I'm assuming you earn as an intern, you will either spend a week's salary getting back to New York, or you will spend the night here at the country club. I can arrange it."

"No thanks. I'll manage," said Stephen.

"There is another solution. I'm going into the city this evening. I can give you a lift."

"That's very generous of you, but no thank you. I"ll figure something out."

"My grandfather was serious when he said that he wants you in his office at nine. You won't be in any condition to tangle with him if you do not get a good night's sleep, and I can assure you, apart from hitchhiking, you won't be able to return to the city this evening without incurring a sizable expense."

Stephen sighed. "Well, at least I can pay you for your gas and trouble."

"No trouble at all," reassured Jonathan.

The valet brought Jonathan's navy BMW convertible to the entrance. A rather large instrument case occupied the passenger's seat.

"I hope that you don't mind sharing the seat with Mitzi," said Jonathan.

"Mitzi?"

"Mitzi is my mistress. I keep her in a cello case," said Jonathan playfully.

Stephen squeezed into the seat with the massive, encased cello on his lap.

"This is very kind of you. You can let me off at the bridge. I can get a subway from there."

"Nonsense, Stephen Lawrence. I assure you that I am going your way."

"You don't know where I am going," answered Stephen.

"Don't I?" answered Jonathan whimsically.

The sprightly convertible darted down the dark, secluded road.

Chapter IV

Courtney Brielle, long and slender like her brother, Winston, retained a youthful figure as she entered middle age; in point of fact, she seemed to defy the aging process and looked ten or more years younger than her chronological age. Enthusiasm, vitality, and an unwillingness to cut her shoulder-length chestnut hair were instrumental in retarding the appearance of middle age.

"All right, Guy, tell Grandpa what you learned today," said Courtney positioning Guy before Winston, who sat at his cluttered brown, maple desk in the den.

"Good morning, Mrs. Greshman," said Guy with a bow. "My name is Guy François Brielle. My name is pronounced Ghee, but most people call me Guy. I am five years old. I know my colors, my ABCs, and I can count to one-hundred. When I grow up, I want to be a bullfighter."

"A matador," whispered Courtney.

"Oh, that's right, a matador," asserted Guy confidently after the flawless, animated delivery.

"Well," said Winston proudly, "you've certainly remembered a lot, Guy, but I'm a little confused. I thought that you wanted to be a pilot."

"Grandpa, that was last week," sighed Guy impatiently.

Winston smiled, "Oh, my mistake. The week before that it was a scientist, wasn't it?"

"Guy is exercising his options," added Courtney cheerfully.

"Just don't become a dentist," muttered Winston.

"After I'm a matador, I'm going to be a typhoon, like daddy."

"Tycoon," corrected Courtney.

Winston's face darkened. "What made you think of your father, Guy?" asked Winston cautiously.

"I always think of Daddy," chirped Guy.

"Sheridon phoned last night," said Courtney apprehensively.

"Why wasn't I informed?" asked Winston with mounting irritation.

"You were asleep; we didn't want to waken you. He's coming for a visit." Courtney braced herself for the impending fireworks.

"Hooray! Daddy's coming!" cheered Guy.

"When will this event take place?" asked Winston straining to hide his displeasure.

Courtney shook her head. "I don't know. He has to attend to some business matters in New York sometime this month and plans to stop by for a visit."

"We'll all wait on pins and needles," said Winston sarcastically, "for the supreme visit from His Royal Majesty."

"Don't you want Daddy to come, Grandpa?" asked Guy touching the model of *David* that adorned Winston's desk. Winston moved the sixteen-inch alabaster replica of Michelangelo's masterpiece away from Guy's inquisitive fingers.

"I won't break it, Grandpa, I promise," assured Guy.

"I know, Guy, but *David* is fragile. Your fingers have oils that might stain the finish. Winston positioned *David* on the other end of the desk and placed a peppermint in Guy's disappointed hands.

"Listen, Guy," said Courtney, "it's the ice cream truck."

Guy's eyes sparkled. "I want strawberry ice! Come on, Aunt Courtney." Guy tugged at Courtney's hand and pulled her towards the front door. As the door opened, they stood face to face with a tall, imposing presence.

"Sheridon," whispered Courtney in utter amazement.

Sheridon Southgate kissed his Aunt Courtney's cheek. "Aunt Courtney, you're looking as lovely as ever."

Guy gazed up into the eyes of his father.

"You must be Guy." Sheridon lifted his son and held him in his arms. Guy hugged his father's neck and wrapped his legs around his waist. They remained entwined for a few moments. "You're just as I imagined—a chip off the old block, if I must say so myself," said Sheridon proudly.

"Isn't this a touching scene," said Winston sarcastically as he approached the door.

"Hello, Dad." Sheridon placed Guy down gently. The youth stared up at his father as the sound of the ice cream bell tinkled away in the distance. "Don't worry, I'll take you for ice cream later," reassured Sheridon.

"We haven't seen you in three years. You hardly write or call, and if Guy wasn't standing in the doorway, you wouldn't be able to point him out in a lineup," reprimanded Winston.

"As diplomatic as ever, I see. May I come in?" asked Sheridon politely.

"Of course," said Courtney taking Sheridon's hand. Guy held Sheridon's other hand and walked proudly with his father into the living room.

Winston closed the door. "I want to know why all of a sudden you show up in the doorway without any warning."

"Warning?" chuckled Sheridon. "Am I the plague?"

"If you aren't, you're darned close to it!" bellowed Winston. "Well, you didn't answer my question. What are you doing here out of the clear, blue sky?"

Sheridon's gaze left his son's cherub face and rested upon his agitated father. "I wanted to see you, Aunt Courtney, and my son, Dad."

"Why? Are you dying or something?" asked Winston angrily.

"Winston!" scolded Courtney. "I'm sorry, Sheridon. Winston, look at what you're doing to Guy."

Guy trembled nervously and tugged at his father's arm.

"Daddy, look what I can do." Guy recited his introduction to his teacher, but this time, it was neither flawless nor animated.

"That's great, Guy," said Sheridon enthusiastically. "What's this all about?"

"Your son is preparing to enter kindergarten. Of course, you wouldn't know that," said Winston sardonically.

"Will you come to school with me to meet my teacher, Daddy?" asked Guy hopefully.

Sheridon sighed. "September is four months away, Guy.

Winston smirked.

"But I will be a part of your life," promised Sheridon. "I won't be away from you."

"How do you plan to manage that?" inquired Winston. "You live on another continent, and don't tell me that you're thinking of moving here. I won't see Guy shuttled around from nanny to nanny while you go traipsing all over the globe putting people out of business. Do you think I haven't read about you? You're a vicious scavenger, and there isn't a day that goes by that I don't wonder how a predator like you could ever have come from your mother's womb."

Guy watched both men curiously. "Aunt Courtney, what's a predator?" inquired Guy.

"All right, you two, that's enough," said Courtney taking Guy's hand. "I'm taking Guy out for a walk."

"I want to stay here with Daddy!" cried Guy.

"I'll be right here when you get back," consoled Sheridon. "I promise."

Guy and Courtney started for the door. Guy looked back at his father and grandfather with apprehension.

"Come along, Guy," said Courtney leading him out of the door.

Sheridon watched his son and aunt walk down the sunny, tree-lined street.

"I can remember when you took me out for strolls when you came to visit Grandfather Southgate's house. Of course, it was after the shouting match. Some things never change," said Sheridon.

"Spare me the stroll down memory lane," said Winston angrily. The thought of Herman Southgate made his blood chill. "What do you want, Sheridon?"

Sheridon looked at his father. Winston's eyes seemed tired, and his body appeared frail. Sheridon sighed. "Dad, I'm married. My wife's name is Kate. You have a granddaughter, Taylor."

"When did all of this happen?" asked Winston calming himself.

"Does it really matter? The bottom line is that I'm settled. My family and I live very comfortably in England. Taylor and Guy are brother and sister; I want them to be together. I want Guy to return to England with me to live with his family."

Winston smiled and shook his head in disbelief. "I haven't seen you in three years, and you have the temerity to waltz in here and announce that you have a wife and daughter in England, and you want to take Guy back with you. Let me give *you* the bottom line, Sheridon. My grandson is not leaving this house to live in some English country house with a bunch of strangers."

"We're his family, Dad," explained Sheridon.

"Oh, pardon me, a family of strangers." Winston's eyes pierced his son's tranquil face. "You're a real Southgate, aren't you? It doesn't matter who you hurt. It's all about your sense of entitlement and privilege. I may not have your money, and we don't live in a country house, but this is Guy's home, and he's not leaving."

Winston walked to the window and looked out upon the children playing kickball in the quiet street. "I can't fault you," reflected Winston. "You were raised with Southgate pretensions. I turned you over to those fiends; I can't complain about what they made of you. You're selfish, insensitive, and merciless. You've made your money on other people's misfortune— misfortune that you orchestrate. Guy is not going to become a part of that world."

Sheridon placed an envelope in Winston's hand. "This says that he is."

"What is this?" asked Winston noticing the return address of a New York law firm.

"You never bothered to file for custody, Dad. This document grants full custody to me."

"That's absurd!" yelled Winston. "You can't do that."

"I don't want to fight you, Dad. Please, be reasonable. Your retirement dinner is in a couple of months. I have your health records here." Sheridon produced another envelope from his jacket pocket. "You've had three heart attacks within the past five years, and you require heart surgery now."

Winston snatched the envelope from Sheridon's hands and ripped it open.

"Where did you get all of this?"

"It doesn't matter, Dad."

Winston looked incredulously at his son. "You knew about the heart attacks, and you didn't call, write, or come to visit?"

"Believe me, Dad. I had the situation monitored carefully. I knew that my presence would upset you. Be reasonable. Aunt Courtney has taken three leaves of absence from her job in order to care for Guy. I know that the school district is forcing you to retire because of your health problems," said Sheridon drifting into the tone he oftentimes reserved for shattered businessmen who had lost their fortunes to him as he convinced them that the takeover was in their best interest. "If Guy comes with me, you can have the operation you need and recuperate afterwards without any cares. When you're strong enough, Kate and I hope that you will consider moving in with us. That way, you can be close to both of your grandchildren."

"Get out of my house," said Winston softly. He walked weakly to the sofa and sat down holding the documents on his lap.

"I promised Guy that I would be here when he returned. I'm going to keep my promise, Dad. I'll wait out on the sidewalk if I must, but I will keep my promise. I will keep all of my promises," proclaimed Sheridon.

A tired, silent Winston sat on the sofa and watched the back of his strong, virile son as he stood at the window waiting for Guy. Visions of Bambi came to mind as the fully-grown buck stood proudly on top of the mountain, and his father stepped down, relinquishing control to his son. Winston and Sheridon watched the remastered "Bambi" movie countless times; it was Sheridon's favorite Disney movie. Winston marveled at how closely art imitated life, only in this imitation, Bambi shoves his father off of the mountaintop and assumes his position at the apex by force. Dear Reader, only Shakespeare can provide reasoning for this dramatic tragedy:

How sharper than a serpent's tooth it is
To have a thankless child!

Chapter V

Television monitors glared overhead and blasted the latest financial reports from the Stock Exchange. Arnold closed his office door and stared at the blank computer screen on his desk. Technology surrounded him, much to his chagrin. The stress that enveloped the air at the start of each new day seemed to invigorate his employees, but Arnold longed for a time when computers, laptops, and other wireless gadgets were contained within the realms of science fiction. Perhaps it *was* time to retire. There were villas in Tuscany calling to him whenever meetings became tedious or when traffic jarred his frazzled nerves or when cell phones jangled incessantly. There were always solutions. James was a competent driver and could maneuver the traffic on the George Washington Bridge like a munitions expert on the battlefield. *Zach.* The most salient problem offered no solution and was going to meet with him at 9AM. Daniel Cohen was a dutiful son, but he lacked the business acumen needed to head a multi-million dollar corporation. True, Arnold could run the corporation from a distant, tranquil locale, but with Daniel at the helm, the word *respite* would be an oxymoron. Better to wait it out. In five years, perhaps Daniel would be tempted to leave New York and establish a residence in Paris, at the incessant urging of Elizabeth, the frustrated designer who gave up her promising career in order to be a never stay-at-home wife. Elizabeth's hosiery designs drew mounting interest in the fickle world of 1976 haute couture, and she never let her husband forget it. According to her calculations, she would have been a name fit to be uttered on the tongues of every chic Park Avenue debutante had she not been saddled with a husband and two children. It was no consolation to Elizabeth that Sara had no interest in fashion, and Jonathan, a meticulous dresser with a keen fashion instinct, shunned high society and buried himself behind a cumbersome cello. Arnold reflected upon the fourteen-room home on the North Shore he helped Daniel purchase for Elizabeth and realized that the couple would be anchored in New York indefinitely.

"They're waiting for you in the conference room, Arnold," said a mature, stable voice at the door.

"Good morning, Simmons, and how was your evening?"

Simmons, Arnold's senior executive, smiled. Simmons was Arnold's most trusted employee and valued friend, second only to the friendship Arnold managed to maintain with his childhood friend, Winston Brielle.

"I heard about the fracas last night," said Simmons. " I can't say that I'm sorry I missed it."

"What's this about the conference room? I'm meeting Daniel and Lawrence here in my office at nine." Arnold checked his watch. "It's only eight ten. I've never known my son to be early for a meeting, at which it is assured that I will chastise him severely."

Simmons' smile widened. "I think that you might want to attend this meeting, Arnold. Daniel has a grand surprise awaiting you."

"Well, I commend his enthusiasm. I can fire him in the conference room as well as in my office." Arnold led the way to the conference room at the end of the corridor; Simmons walked towards the elevator. "Where are you going?" asked Arnold. "I thought that you said they were in the conference room.".

"They are in Conference Room East, Arnold," replied Simmons with a vague smile. "Conference Room East is on the eighty-second floor."

Arnold's expression was one of incredulity.

"Am I to understand that we have another conference room towards the east?" asked Arnold.

Simmons smiled as they entered the elevator and disembarked on the eighty-second floor.

"You *are* aware that we are heading north, aren't you?" asked a perplexed Arnold as they walked down the corridor.

Simmons retained his composure silently.

Chapter VI

Arnold stood in utter amazement as he viewed the massive expansion of Cohen Unlimited on the eighty-second floor. Simmons led the CEO through a large area staffed with formally attired, eager, young executives. All seemed smitten with their computer screens, cell phones, and other technological devices that were only minimally present in the corporate offices on the fifty-seventh floor. The overhead monitors reported the inescapable Dow, NAS, and S&P reports.

"Where is my son?" asked Arnold harnessing his impending rage.

Simmons knocked gently on an elegantly carved oak door with the company's insignia emblazoned in Edwardian Script gold letters. Arnold stood in awe as the door opened. Daniel rushed to greet his father.

"Welcome to our new offices, Dad. Come over here and sit at the head of the table. It was going to be a surprise for your retirement, something like a departing gift. Cohen Unlimited will be the envy of every corporation in town. Well, what do you think?"

Arnold scrutinized the room. The panoramic view of the New York skyline was magnificent. A mahogany bar, fully stocked, graced the left corner. White Corinthian columns stood watch unobtrusively from the four corners of the room. A crystal chandelier, oppressively large and resplendent, held court over the center of the elongated, mahogany conference table. European art adorned the walls. Arnold gasped as he viewed a replica of Michelangelo's *Creation* painted upon the ceiling.

"You're speechless, Dad. I knew that you would be. Well, what do you think?"

Arnold sat in a white Louis XV chair near the entrance to gather his wits. Simmons bent over the chair and whispered, "You won't believe what is at the end of the hall."

Arnold's eyes labored to view the spectacle. At the far end of the hall stood a life-sized model of *Venus di Milo* at the entrance of an ornate bathroom, complete with fourteen caret gold fixtures. Arnold closed his eyes. Simmons tried to shield his amusement by placing his hand over his smiling lips.

"Who are these people?" asked Arnold wearily surveying the young executives seated around the conference table. The group, all under the age of thirty-five and of diverse ethnicities, seemed oblivious to his presence. Their laptops were poised before their eager fingers and vibrating cell phones kept the room abuzz.

"This is our team, Dad," said Daniel proudly. "They're the sharpest minds in the Western hemisphere, and they are all working with us."

Arnold's face reddened, and his heart beat furiously. "Is that right?" asked Arnold calmly.

"Yes," beamed Daniel.

"Why wasn't I consulted about any of this?" asked Arnold quietly.

"Come now, Dad, after your gift to Sara, I assumed that consultation was a useless form of communication here at Cohen Unlimited."

Arnold looked at his son steadfastly. "Sara's gift was issued last night; this fiasco has been in the offing for quite some time. There's no way you could have pulled this off on your own. I don't see Lawrence. Why isn't he here with the other illustrious minds?"

"Jonathan took Stephen to an antique show," said Daniel.

"Simmons, get my grandson on the phone! Tell him that I want Lawrence in my office before noon." Arnold addressed the group. "Ladies and gentlemen, and I use the terms loosely, this meeting is adjourned."

"Are we meeting at another location?" asked a young man with a cell phone to his ear.

"I'll thank you to remove that obstruction from your face before addressing me," huffed Arnold.

The young man concluded his conversation and closed the flip-top cell phone abruptly. "

"There will be no further meetings," continued Arnold. "This group is disbanded."

"Until further notice," intoned Daniel.

"Permanently!" barked Arnold. "I don't want to see any of your faces on these premises again."

"I'm afraid you can't do that," replied a voice calmly. "We've all made substantial investments in various projects…"

"I advise you to tread cautiously, Mr. Southgate. I know your history of takeovers and mergers. My high regard for your family will not prevent me from grinding you into the dust if you try to employ any of that nonsense here."

"We stand to lose millions if we back out now, Arnold," argued Sheridon.

"Mr. Cohen!" yelled Arnold.

"Sorry, Mr. Cohen it is," said Sheridon. "We've all made sizable investments. Surely you don't expect us to walk away now."

"*Run* would be a better word, Mr. Southgate," warned Arnold.

A female voice entered the discourse. Arnold was not accustomed to female voices at conference meetings. "Mr. Cohen, please be reasonable," entreated the voice. "We can turn a profit in a matter of days..."

"Young woman, perhaps you did not hear me," said Arnold slowly. "This meeting is adjourned. You vultures can seek your prey elsewhere. Now, please, remove yourselves from the premises before I phone security to have you removed forcibly. Now, if you will excuse me, the terminations will begin immediately, beginning with the one in my office." Arnold cast a chilling glance at Daniel as the group exited the elaborate conference room.

• • •

Daniel's hands trembled with agitation as he stood before his father's old-fashioned desk. The elder Cohen turned on his dated computer.

"You made me look foolish up there," lamented Daniel.

"Simmons!" yelled Arnold. Simmons appeared in the doorway. "Did you reach my grandson?"

"We reached him in Montreal," said Simmons. He and Mr. Lawrence will be returning for the noon meeting."

"What's he doing in Montreal?" asked Arnold in utter confusion.

"It seems that the antique shop is in Montreal," explained Simmons. "I've been instructed to tell you that Mr. Cohen is bringing you a gift that you will find intriguing.

"Simmons, find out how much those offices on the eighty-second floor are costing us," said Arnold." If the cost is reasonable, keep them, but get rid of the people up there and bring in our own staff. Get a decorator who understands that a place of business should look like a place of business. I want Winslow Homer up there, and I don't want him on the ceiling."

Simmons smiled. "Yes, sir, will there be anything else?"

"Yes, prepare termination papers for my son," asserted Arnold.

"You can't fire me!" shrieked Daniel. "Grandfather wanted me here. He stipulated it in his will."

"Your grandfather did not intend for you to bring the Louvre and the Sistine Chapel into the office," huffed Arnold. " You are quite right. I cannot fire you, but I can place you on leave of absence until further notice."

"It is 2001, Dad. Cohen Unlimited must keep pace with the Twenty-First Century. We need to form partnerships with other investors, and we need to take advantage of the technological advances that are driving our competitors' profits through the roof."

"Go home and think about what you've done. Enjoy your new house and play with your new technological toys, but don't interfere in the company's business. You don't know who you're dealing with. How you can collaborate with Sheridon Southgate in any business endeavor is beyond me. He'll skin you alive and trade your bones to the highest bidder. You don't know those people, Son, but, rest assured, they know you. Now leave while I'm in a good mood."

"What about Stephen, Dad? Please don't fire him. He was only following orders."

"Perhaps Mr. Lawrence should learn that the first order of business is to know who gives the orders. I'm still CEO around here; henceforth, he'll take orders from me. Get rid of any ridiculous notions about pairing him up with Sara. We've seen the side of the road upon which Mr. Lawrence likes to drive."

"What do you mean?" asked Daniel innocently. "So he visited an antique shop in Montreal with Jonathan. Jonathan can be persuasive and imperial, Dad, you know that. Stephen tries not to offend anyone."

Arnold sighed and returned to his computer.

•   •   •

Stephen Lawrence hastened to the elevator and pressed the up button. How ironic. Twenty-four hours ago, the intern's professional life was ascending. Now, like the descending elevator, it was taking a downward turn. Jonathan touched Stephen's rigid arm.

"Relax, my grandfather is reasonable and has a tremendous sense of the ridiculous," confided Jonathan as they stepped onto the elevator.

"I think that I should see him alone," said Stephen nervously.

"I won't hear of it. Look at you. You're trembling at the thought of facing him; my grandfather detests weakness. I shall come along and smooth things over. I have a special gift," said Jonathan confidently.

Stephen's life had been altered dramatically with the advent of Jonathan Cohen. The imperious new acquaintance controlled and manipulated people as easily as he manipulated the strings of his cello.

"What do we tell him? asked Stephen anxiously.

"We'll tell him the truth, of course," asserted Jonathan forthrightly as they exited the elevator.

Stephen hesitated. "I'm not comfortable with this, Jonathan."

"Are you not comfortable with the truth?" asked Jonathan smiling.

"You know what I mean," answered Stephen as they started down the corridor.

"Relax and leave everything to me," said Jonathan. "We will tell him of our intentions."

Stephen hesitated again. "What intentions?"

"We will live together, of course, for the duration of the summer. I must say, Stephen, you evince little imagination," said Jonathan as they walked slowly down the corridor.

"What happens after the summer?" asked Stephen. There was no response. Stephen shook his head slowly as he followed Jonathan into Arnold Cohen's office.

Arnold sat calmly at his desk and watched his grandson and the company intern as they neared his office. Jonathan sauntered into the open door and sat on the brown leather sofa; Stephen stood timidly outside of the door waiting to be asked to enter.

"Come inside, Stephen. He doesn't bite," reassured Jonathan.

"I wouldn't be too sure of that," said Arnold briskly. "What are you doing here, Jonathan? I told Lawrence to come alone."

"Call him Stephen, Grandfather. He's almost a part of the family." Jonathan placed a box covered in gold wrapping paper on Arnold's desk. "I brought you a gift."

"This is no time for gifts, Jonathan. I want to speak with Lawrence alone. Why are you standing in the doorway, Lawrence? Come in and sit down."

Stephen entered timidly and sat at the far end of the sofa.

"You must open our present to you," persisted Jonathan.

Arnold tore the wrapping paper off of the gift impatiently and tossed it to the floor. His expression softened. "What is this?" asked Arnold quietly.

"Do you not recognize it, Grandfather? It is the medallion Uncle Zach's platoon won for bravery. You mentioned that you would try to retrieve it from the veteran selling it on the Internet."

Arnold took the medallion from the box gingerly. "Where did you get this?" asked Arnold without diverting his attention from the medallion.

"The veteran lives in Montreal. I hastened there before he had an opportunity to finalize any sales on the Internet. Stephen went along to keep me company. You are pleased with our gift, are you not? Surely, you won't be too harsh with Stephen in light of our intentions, will you Grandfather?"

Arnold held the medallion tightly in his hands.

Stephen colored; his hands trembled.

"The veteran has fallen upon hard times; I issued a generous check to him and his family. I knew that you would be pleased," said Jonathan moving closer to Stephen on the sofa.

"I'm sorry, Sir," said Stephen with genuine remorse. "I missed the meeting and let the corporation down."

"Nonsense," said Jonathan. "I am a part of the corporation, and you haven't let me down. In point of fact, I feel rather uplifted."

"I'm sorry for my actions, Sir. I assure you that it won't happen again. I hope that you will give me an opportunity to prove that I…"

"Stephen and I would like to head a Summer Initiatives Program in the new offices on the eighty-second floor," said Jonathan. "I've already contacted alumni interested in helping to get the programs afloat."

"What are you talking about?" asked Arnold placing the medallion on his desk. "What Summer Initiatives Program, and are you telling me that you knew about the offices on the eighty-second floor?"

"Of course, "said Jonathan matter-of-factly. "Mother decorated them with those grievous paintings and replicas. I dare say, Grandfather, you are probably the only one who did not know."

Arnold looked out of the window and sighed. "Perhaps it is time for retirement."

"Nonsense, Grandfather. You're simply too focused on the microcosm; today's market requires a panoramic vista. That is where Stephen and I come in. We bring youth, vitality, and vision to Cohen Unlimited. The Summer Initiatives Program can expose under-developed communities to the technology they need to advance in today's techno-society. I was thinking of adopting a school, providing computers, and preparing industrious youth for careers in corporate America."

Stephen looked at Jonathan with amazement. Arnold's gaze remained upon the medallion upon his desk. "You know that it is a good idea, Grandfather, and it will be a perfect tax write-off to offset some of the expense of that horrid extravaganza you refer to as Conference Room East."

Arnold studied at his grandson. There was a meeting of the minds. Where father and son disconnected, grandfather and grandson connected. "I like the idea of community involvement," said Arnold.

"Of course, you do. You have a heart to help people. At the conclusion of the program, we can evaluate its strengths and ascertain whether or not it merits further development. There is one stipulation—Stephen and I head the programs. We envision environmental and wildlife programs in addition to the computer program."

"And you think that you and Lawrence can handle all of this?" asked Arnold.

"Of course," replied Jonathan. "During our trip to Montreal, I learned many things about Stephen. Although the trip ended far too soon, I think that I know Stephen well enough to assure you that he is up to the task."

"It might work," said Arnold thoughtfully. "There won't be anything for Lawrence to do around here. Your father is on leave of absence until further notice."

Stephen felt like an insignificant integer as grandfather and grandson spoke about him in the abstract. Arnold stood. "All right, we'll give it a try."

"We'll take care of everything, Grandfather. I've already contacted a friend at UC Berkeley, who is a superb interior decorator. We'll re-design those offices to reflect our new vision."

"All right, but Simmons will oversee the operation and report back to me. The idea has merit. Now, I would like to take your grandmother out for lunch and get away from all of this for awhile." Arnold patted his grandson on the back. "Good work."

"I will never disappoint you, Grandfather, never," assured Jonathan.

•   •   •

"You didn't ask me. What if I don't want to be involved with Summer Initiative Programs?" asked Stephen as he walked with Jonathan to the elevator.

"Don't be absurd," said Jonathan. "Without my quick thinking, you would have been fired. You are now the head of innovative corporate programs instead of my father's lackey."

"Your father had good ideas. I felt that I was involved with something important," said Stephen.

"You were involved with activities that would have bankrupted this corporation and made us prime for takeover and legal action. I don't think that would be a welcomed addition to your resume. Trust me, Stephen. You are in good hands," assured Jonathan.

"How do you know so much about it? I thought that your interest was in music," said Stephen.

"You are upset, but business is not the cause," observed Jonathan. "I will answer your initial question. I don't know what will happen when the summer ends. Isn't that the joy of life—the unpredictable? Let us enjoy one another for the time we share together. The future will take care of itself." Stephen entered the elevator with Jonathan, who viewed life as a tremendous cello; Stephen was merely the bow he used to enliven the strings.

Chapter VII

Susannah Cohen played the message again. Her hand trembled as she heard Joshua's voice, a voice that was not as she recalled. Joshua's tone was impatient with a tinge of antagonism. Susannah listened again and determined that the muffled sound of the television, the occasional bark of a dog, and the quiet voices in the background indicated that her son had a family. The message was succinct and informative. Richard Winwood, ex-marine and ex-husband, had died. The distant voice offered details of funeral arrangements and the like, but it offered no warmth, no recognition, and no interest in the recipient of the call.

Richard Winwood returned from Vietnam two years before the war ended. The diagnosis was manic depression and signaled the end of a brilliant surgeon's career. The disorder catapulted into a lamentable conclusion to a fifteen-year marriage. To the sensitive teenager, Joshua Winwood, Arnold Cohen, and not Richard Winwood's depression, destroyed his parent's marriage. In truth, Richard Winwood's mental condition placed his marriage on tenuous grounds long before Susannah met Arnold, but, Dear Reader, the truth is not always a welcomed visitor.

Susannah re-played the message and thought of Joshua's last words to her when she told him of her decision to end her marriage, to resurrect her medical studies, and to marry her college sweetheart. Joshua's words were harsh and filled with derision; that notwithstanding, Susannah married Arnold and graduated from medical school. Arnold was attentive, loving, and supportive; Susannah enjoyed an idyllic marriage.

As Arnold's car pulled up in the driveway, Susannah played the message once more and resolved to attend the funeral services of Richard Winwood and discover the branch of her family living in San Francisco that she had never known.

Upon entering the bedroom, Arnold found Susannah still dressed in her nightgown listening to the answering machine recording.

"I thought that we were having lunch," said Arnold.

Susannah played the recording for her husband.

"I want to attend," said Susannah softly. Her eyes looked at her husband imploringly.

Arnold turned away. "That might not be a good idea. It doesn't sound as though Joshua wants you to come."

"Still, I must go."

"Must?"

"I owe him at least that."

"You owe him nothing. You have a home here. Joshua has made a life for himself out there. Let it remain as it is, Susannah. You can't bring the dead back to life. You will only cause misery for yourself and open old wounds."

Susannah remained silent.

"What about your patients?" reasoned Arnold. "Do you plan to leave them?"

"Reynolds can substitute for me. This is important, Arnold. How often do I ask for anything?"

"You never ask for anything," said Arnold.

"Well, I'm asking for this," replied Susannah remorsefully.

"And if I do not concur with your wishes?"

"I will go," Susannah said softly. "I owe him that."

"You owe him nothing," remarked Arnold trying to conceal his anger.

"Joshua is my son. Whether he wants me there or not, I will be there. I heard voices in the background. I think that he has a family. I may be a grandmother to children that I have never met. I want to meet them. I want to know them. I must go, Arnold," said Susannah urgently.

Arnold sighed and held his wife close to his heart. "Then we will go, but I'm telling you that it is a mistake. He doesn't want us there."

Susannah rested upon Arnold's shoulder. The idyllic marriage did not falter.

Chapter IIX

Joshua Cohen stood proudly beside the flag-draped coffin of his father. Two marines attired in full dress uniform removed, folded, and placed the American flag into Joshua's steady hands. Arnold tried to remember Joshua as a child, but his thoughts were vague and blurred. Now, Joshua stood as a man beside his deceased father's coffin. Two young adults stood near Joshua's wife. It occurred to Arnold that he and Susannah had grandchildren that they had never met. Ironically, they seemed to be the same age as Jonathan and Sara. The boy comforted his sister as they walked past the mourners assembled at the Veteran's Cemetery. Susannah hoped that Joshua would glance in her direction, but he looked straight ahead, helped his wife and children into the limousine, and did not look back.

"Give him time," consoled Arnold. "We'll contact them before we leave."

"He wouldn't even look at me," said Susannah soberly.

"Joshua has a lot on his mind right now. Tomorrow will be better," said Arnold.

Arnold led Susannah to their rented car and helped her in. A group of handicapped veterans, Richard's friends, entered a white van in front of the car. The veterans, in dress uniform, maneuvered their wheelchairs into the van. Arnold's eyes rested on the double amputee with steel-blue eyes. Their glances locked briefly; the veteran looked away.

"Why were you staring?" asked Susannah. "I think that you made those men uncomfortable, Arnold."

"I couldn't help it. The last one on the van reminded me of someone."

"Still, it was impolite to stare," said Susannah.

The funeral party allowed the veteran's van to exit first. Arnold watched the van pull off. The veteran with the steel-blue eyes turned and looked back at Arnold as the van turned the corner.

"Did you get the name on the van?" asked Arnold. "Perhaps I can make a donation."

"The cars are beginning to move," said Susannah. " Let's go. I can't bear to be here any longer."

Arnold waited patiently until he could maneuver out of the space into the long procession of cars. The piercing blue eyes of the handicapped veteran were emblazoned within his consciousness. Arnold wondered in which war the man had received his debilitating injuries.

"What if we stayed a little longer?" he asked a now controlled Susannah. "In a few days, Joshua might be amenable to a meeting."

"No, let's leave tomorrow as planned," said Susannah. " I would like to meet my grandchildren under better circumstances. We can come back in a couple of weeks."

"A couple of weeks might be too late," said Arnold anxiously.

"Too late for what?" asked Susannah. "Arnold, you're not thinking of tracking down that poor man on the van, are you?"

"Of course not, we'll leave tomorrow," said Arnold.

The car inched out of the parking space into the procession and moved slowly with the flow of traffic. Zachery Cohen's penetrating, steel-blue eyes gazed with relief out of the window of the veteran's van as it moved along the highway unencumbered.

Chapter IX

Courtney, Sheridon, and Guy Brielle sat on the top deck of the Circle Line as it glided through the murky waters of the Hudson River. The afternoon sun shone with a compassion that allowed the passengers to admire the New York skyline without the rays of the sun scorching their bodies mercilessly. Guy napped peacefully on his father's lap. A full day of sightseeing exhausted the exuberant youth. Courtney and Sheridon sat in silence avoiding the inevitable discussion of Guy's departure.

"Why is it you never married, Aunt Courtney? You're beautiful and vibrant. Surely there are men in New York who can provide you with a life of leisure and ease," said Sheridon.

Courtney smiled. "Is that what life is to you, Sheridon—leisure and ease?"

"You know what I mean? You shouldn't have to work and be a constant companion to my father. Haven't you ever wanted a life of your own?"

"Sheridon, you amaze me. You are an educated man, but you know so little."

"How so?"

"You married because it was convenient," explained Courtney. "You needed a wife in order to prosper in the corporate world and justify taking Guy away from the only home he has known."

"That doesn't explain why you never married."

"No, it doesn't. Perhaps I'm waiting for that special someone."

"There has never been a special someone?" asked Sheridon.

"There is always a special someone," reasoned Courtney. "Sometimes, it just isn't convenient."

"Zachary Cohen is dead. You must move on, Aunt Courtney," advised Sheridon.

Courtney's breath caught in her throat.

"You've spent your whole life dreaming of what cannot be, when there are so many men out there waiting to give you the life you deserve," said Sheridon.

Sheridon reached into his pocket without disturbing Guy and produced a picture of his wife and daughter. "That's Kate, my wife, and Taylor, your niece."

Courtney took the picture and studied it carefully.

"This could be a picture of your family, if you would allow yourself to embrace life."

Courtney studied the thick, red hair of her niece and the docile expression of her sister-in-law.

"She's the image of your mother, you know," said Courtney gently.

"Do you think so? Of course, I've only seen pictures of my mother. Grandfather Southgate kept my mother's pictures locked in a drawer in his den. I've never seen any in Dad's house."

"Winston keeps them out of sight also. Chloe was a painful loss." Courtney gazed at the picture. "Now, here she is staring from a distant shore."

"Aunt Courtney, that picture is of my daughter, not my mother. My mother is a part of the past, a past that I have never known. It is a past that I do not care to revisit."

"You cannot control the past. It speaks its own language," said Courtney.

"I can't do anything about the past, Aunt Courtney, no one can, but I can do something about the present," assured Sheridon.

"You mean control the present?" asked Courtney.

"I want to tuck Guy and Taylor in at night and show them the world," said Sheridon convincingly.

"Has Winston seen this picture?" asked Courtney gazing at the mischievous smile of the freckled lass.

"No, he hasn't given me an opportunity to share my life with him," said Sheridon.

"That's because your life requires a dismantling of his," informed Courtney.

"What would you have me do, Aunt Courtney? Have I not the right to be a father to my children?" asked Sheridon.

"Let me show him the picture," said Courtney softly with a sigh. "Winston may lose Guy, but if he can be flexible, he may be able to see his precious Chloe in this little lady's lovely face."

"That may be a short-term solution, but it won't help in the long-term. I don't want Dad to see the past in Taylor. I want him to see the future. My father can live a life of comfort and joy with me and his grandchildren, if he would only be reasonable and explore the possibilities. I want you and Dad to return to England with me. Your life in English society will be the type of life you deserve. We can be a family, the kind of family my father has always wanted. It can happen, Aunt Courtney. I can make it happen," asserted Sheridon.

Courtney smiled. "Sheridon, you are a master crafter. You've built a financial empire with mergers and acquisitions, and now you want to build a family using the same techniques. Your father will never move to England, and he will not permit you to return with Guy."

"Then he will experience a hell that he cannot even imagine," said Sheridon.

"Sheridon, what are you saying?" asked Courtney with trepidation.

"I am saying that nothing will prevent me from taking Guy to England to be with his family," said Sheridon.

"You are willing to destroy your father?" Courtney asked incredulously.

Sheridon considered briefly. "It is my hope that my father will place Guy's needs above his own."

"He will fight you," admonished Courtney.

"Then he will lose. Talk to him, Aunt Courtney, please. Help me to make all of our lives better."

Courtney looked at Guy sleeping on his father's lap and realized that she was entering a world where peace was an unnecessary byproduct. It was a cold, callous world, but it would, most assuredly, be Guy's new world.

Chapter X

Profits were up at Southgate Enterprises, but as history demonstrated time and time again, profits were of a cyclical nature in high-risk tech areas. A period of low returns inevitably followed a period of high returns. Sheridon's team had the utmost confidence in their plans to eliminate at least thirty-thousand jobs in three top American corporations, destabilize the New York economy, and initiate the de-merger of Provan Wireless, a key enterprise that Sheridon coveted. A loss of profits in the US economy would precipitate reciprocal losses in the UK economy. The possibility that Southgate Enterprises would suffer losses on both continents was a strong possibility, a possibility Sheridon hoped to extinguish with the acquisition of Cohen Unlimited. The de-merger of Provan Wireless was set to begin in two weeks. The pan-European division would be renamed Bentley Wireless, and the fledgling corporation was scheduled to make its Stock Exchange debut at the end of August. A meeting of shareholders was scheduled in two weeks to vote on the de-merger. Prospectuses would be published within days. Sheridon and his team were set to embark upon an institutional road show designed to place the de-merger in a favorable light. Family would underpin all negotiations. A tacit premium was placed on family stability in high corporate negotiations, particularly in the European market. If one could manage one's family and resources, then one could be entrusted with the resources and visions of a solid, value-centered corporate enterprise like Provan Wireless.

Sheridon's plan to topple Cohen Unlimited's family leadership backfired. Daniel Cohen was an unreliable ally. Sheridon realized this at the outset, but it was worth a try. Arnold Cohen, a close friend of the head of Provan Wireless, would, undoubtedly, fight the de-merger and position himself to assist his friend with viable resources. Family was Arnold Cohen's strong suit, on the one hand, and his harmatia, on the other. Sheridon devoted a great portion of his day pondering links that would weaken or destroy the Cohen family fortress. If he had to take the entire Cohen family down with their corporation, Sheridon would do it, and he was convinced that a melodious cello, a tender smile, and a pair of steel-blue eyes would give him the leverage that he needed.

Chapter XI

The flight attendant stood poised and ready to assist as his colleagues helped the woman move from the seat to her wheelchair. The youthful attendant wondered why an attractive woman would have to endure such a fate. Was it the result of an accident, or was it a malady afflicting her from birth? He smiled and bid her adieu as her caretaker pushed the chair towards the ramp.

"Cheers," said the attendant as the woman passed. She returned the smile but offered no response. The attendant watched her wheelchair proceed down the ramp guided by a statuesque girl trying, in vain, to hold onto a vivacious, russet-haired tyke.

Sheridon Southgate smiled broadly as his wife, daughter, and au pair approached the check-in area. The little girl hastened to greet her father. Sheridon lifted Taylor and held her tightly.

"I missed you, Daddy," said Taylor squeezing her father's neck in a loving embrace.

"I told you that I would see you soon. Didn't you believe me?"

Sheridon kissed Taylor and then bent down to kiss his wife's cheek. "You're going to love New York. I'll bet you're hungry. I'll get you a New York hot dog, Cream Puff."

"No, Daddy, get me ice cream," insisted Taylor.

"Ice cream it shall be. I'll take over here, Iris," said Sheridon placing his hands on the wheelchair. Why don't you take Taylor to the little ladies room before we go to the hotel."

"No, Daddy, I want ice cream!" screamed Taylor.

"Iris, would you, please, see if you can find her an ice cream bar?" asked Sheridon.

"Come along, Taylor." Iris had a lilting voice. She wore her hair in two long braids, which extended beyond her shoulders. Her ebony, glazed skin contrasted sharply with Taylor's ruddy complexion. Sheridon knelt down beside the wheelchair and took his wife's hand. She looked at him with concern.

"Something has happened," whispered Sheridon. "It will only be for a short while. We'll be home in a week or two, I promise."

Kate smiled and held her husband's hand tightly. Sheridon felt at peace when he looked into eyes, which did not judge, and a warm grasp, which did not bind or imprison. This was true family, and Sheridon Brielle counted himself a blessed man.

• • •

Winston sat in his brown leather wing chair watching the little girl's curious fingers touch the features of a desk-sized replica of Michelangelo's *David*. She lifted the statue, the finest in Winston's collection, from the desk. Guy entered the room and gasped.

"Put that down, Taylor! That's Grandpa's *David* statue, and we're not allowed to touch it. Isn't that right, Grandpa?" asked Guy.

Winston's eyes did not leave the youthful redhead. "It's all right, Guy. Taylor is just curious."

Guy looked askance at his grandfather. The statue was off limits, at least it had always been for him. Iris, the au pair, entered the den.

"No, Taylor, you must not touch that!" She removed the statue from Taylor's inquisitive fingers and replaced it upon the desk. "Come along, Taylor, it is time for your bath."

"I don't want to go to bed yet!" wailed the fiery redhead. "Daddy said that I could stay up and play with Grandpa forever."

"Take your bath, Taylor," admonished Guy. "I'll tell Daddy that you're being rude again, and he will come and take you away to the hotel to stay with him."

"I'm staying with Grandpa. Tell me a story, Grandpa," said Taylor making herself comfortable upon Winston's lap.

"You have to say please!" shouted Guy. What manner of sister was this? Taylor was the rudest girl that he had ever encountered. "Say please," demanded Guy.

Taylor laughed and snuggled closer to Winston. "Tell me a story about Cuchulainn," said Taylor.

"Who?" asked Winston perplexed.

"Cuchulainn," said Taylor impatiently. "Papa Sean always tells me stories about Cuchulainn.

"I'm sorry, Taylor," said Winston, "I don't know anything about Cuchulainn."

"Make Taylor take her bath, Grandpa," said Guy.

"I have drawn her bath," added Iris. She disliked the manner in which Taylor taunted her brother and manipulated her grandfather. "The water will become tepid."

"We'll just add warm water to it, right, Taylor?" said Winston playfully. He could not remember when he felt so light-hearted.

Guy's vexation was evident as he left the room in a huff.

"Where are you going, Guy? I'm going to tell a story about the three bears. Don't you want to hear it?" asked Winston. "I wonder where that fairy tale book is. It has wonderful pictures. You'll like them, Taylor."

Guy ran to his room, which he now shared with Taylor, and grabbed her favorite companion, a worn teddy bear wearing a tattered Kelly green vest. The sound of splashing water could be heard. Iris investigated.

"Guy, what are you doing?" yelled Iris. Upon entering the bathroom, Iris found Guy shaking Taylor's teddy bear underwater. "Stop that, Guy!" Iris wrestled the soggy bear from the clutches of its adversary. "Look what you've done. It's ruined! Why did you do that, Guy?" Guy laughed as Winston and Taylor entered the bathroom. Taylor began to sob at the sight of her soggy, abused companion. Winston became irate.

"Go to your room, Guy!" yelled Winston.

Guy ran to his room and slammed the door.

"Don't worry, Taylor," consoled Winston. "We'll get you a brand new teddy bear tomorrow."

"I don't want another teddy bear," screamed the inconsolable child. "Papa Sean gave Paddy to me, and Guy killed him!" Taylor grabbed the now droopy bear from Winston's hands and ran out of the room crying.

"I will look after her," said Iris confidently. She was accustomed to Taylor's moods and oftentimes rebellious behavior. The acorn did not fall far from the tree. Iris checked her watch. It was seven o'clock, and she had not yet showered. She felt the envelope in her pocket; it was her passport to freedom in this land of opportunity. Today, she was an au pair, but soon she would be a full-time university student. Her contractual agreement with the Southgate's had been honored, and there had been fringe benefits that she had not anticipated. Sheridon was a generous employer, and she loved the family; however, she was young and life was before her. Iris determined to remain in the Southgate employ for the duration of the summer, but she would not return to England with them in August. She would need time to prepare for her new life as a university student in New York. America's bounteous fruits awaited, and she was eager to claim her share of the harvest.

• • •

Papa Sean. It was the second time that Taylor mentioned his name. Winston knew little about Ireland, and he had no desire to contemplate the distant land. *Papa Sean.* Did Taylor sit on his lap? Who was this Cuchulainn that Papa Sean read stories about to his young granddaughter? For the first time, it occurred to Winston that his granddaughter, the lass with the fiery tresses and obstinate disposition, the beautiful child with the indelible image of his Chloe etched upon her face, belonged to another world—an alien land that he would never know.

Papa Sean, Kate's father, opposed the marriage of his only daughter to *sweet cream.* That was Papa Sean's assessment of Sheridon Southgate. In order to make cream sweet, sugar must be added. At first, the mixture is sweet and velvety, but after a few days, cream and sugar begin to sour and turn yellow. Papa Sean waited for the union of Kate and Sheridon to dissolve, but they seemed happy living in England—the biggest insult of all. Papa Sean did not want his daughter to attend a university in England. There were fine universities in Dublin, but Kate was insistent. She met the crafty American at the university, defied her father, and married Sheridon Southgate. Papa Sean waited for fate to provide the appropriate vengeance for a daughter disobeying her father, but everything Sheridon Southgate touched prospered. When Kate suffered a debilitating stroke while giving birth, Papa Sean forgot all thoughts of vengeance. Taylor entered Papa Sean's world with the force of a fireball. Her brilliant red hair, like his was in younger days, sparkled in the Dublin sun, and her mischievous manner tickled his heart. Papa Sean loved his Taylor, and she spent every summer with him and Grandmother Maureen in Dublin. This summer was the first time that she had ever been parted from him. It did not comfort Papa Sean to know that his beloved fireball would be spending the summer with a strange grandfather across the ocean. His precious, emerald jewel did not belong in England, nor did she belong in the United States. Taylor belonged at home, and home would always be Dublin.

On one side of the Atlantic, one grandfather sat behind a desk in his den gazing wistfully into the twilight as he imagined his granddaughter on the lap of his *adversary.*

On the other side of the Atlantic, another grandfather sat pensively in the pub, tuning out the lilting tunes of the festive singers. Like Siamese twins, Papa Sean and Winston shared one heart—the heart of a fireball. Only death could liberate them.

• • •

Sheridon checked his watch as he sipped a raspberry cappuccino in the Lincoln Center Barnes and Noble café. The ballet would begin in twenty minutes. Where was she? Iris was supposed to say that she was meeting relatives in the city for the evening and meet him at the Barnes and Noble café for a cappuccino before the performance. Sheridon loved the ballet, but Kate did not like to stay up beyond eight o'clock. Dear Reader, I needn't tell you the problems that this arrangement can cause within a marriage, but knowing Kate, the early retirement to her chambers was probably more for Sheridon's benefit than her own. It freed him to enjoy his interests, like the ballet, with companions with full mobility. With an attractive au pair, it would be unnecessary for her husband to meet *companions* at odd hours away from home. As long as they were discreet, Kate was content to read her mysteries and enjoy the comfort of her husband's embrace when he returned to her every night, and he returned to her every night.

Iris was not answering her cell phone. Something was different. Since their arrival to the United States, she seemed distant. Perhaps remaining at Winston's house with Taylor was too much to be expected. Winston's home was small, and Iris was forced to sleep on the sofa bed in the living room. The sofa bed was pulled open, and Iris prepared to slip between the comfort of the paisley cotton sheets when Sheridon appeared in the living room. He looked at the sofa bed with disdain. The living room was hot and humid.

"I'm sorry about this. I don't know why my father won't let me put air-conditioning in this house.

"What are you doing here?" asked Iris quietly. "Someone will hear you."

"You didn't come to the ballet," said Sheridon, "and you weren't answering you cell phone. I thought that something was wrong."

"Why didn't you phone your father? He would have told you that everything was all right." Iris brushed her long, black hair. Sheridon rarely saw it loose around her shoulders. She kept it braided and pinned up to avoid the admiring glances of strangers.

"Why didn't you come? I waited for you." said Sheridon.

"Taylor needed me. There was a disturbance with Guy," answered Iris calmly.

"They will be fine when we go back to England. They don't have room to grow here, and they have few activities that keep them occupied. There's no air-conditioning down here. You shouldn't have to sleep out in the open like this."

Iris welcomed the lack of physical space, for it ensured privacy. Sheridon sat on the edge of the sofa bed.

"I do not think that is wise," said Iris softly.

Sheridon stood up and moved to a green upholstered chair near the sofa bed.

"Do you know that my father had this furniture the last time that I visited him? How many years ago was that?" pondered Sheridon. "I don't know how he can live like this. He won't let me help him."

"Your father is a simple man," explained Iris.

"Unlike his son?"

Iris removed the satiny white robe that Sheridon bought her, for no occasion in particular, and snuggled between the sheets in her green, cotton nightgown.

"I think that you should leave now," said Iris. "Kate will be worried."

"Kate will be fine," said Sheridon.

"Your father might hear you," insisisted Iris.

"Why are you making these excuses? Don't you want to see me? We never have any time together. There are things to be discussed," said Sheridon.

"It is late," said Iris. " We can discuss them in the morning."

"Why are you leaving?" asked Sheridon. He hadn't meant to broach the subject so clumsily, but it was too late.

Iris breathed uneasily.

"I know about the university," said Sheridon.

"I would like to better my life," responded Iris.

"Haven't we given you everything?" asked Sheridon.

"Some things cannot be purchased, Mr. Southgate," answered Iris.

"Everyone's asleep," said Sheridon. "You can speak freely."

"I am speaking freely. From now on, you are Mr. Southgate, even when we are alone," said Iris.

Sheridon could not conceal his angst. "What have I done? Haven't you been happy with us? Have I upset you? Have I failed to please you?"

"You cannot speak this way in your father's house," admonished Iris.

"Tell me! demanded Sheridon incautiously.

"Please lower your voice," said Iris.

"Then tell me what I have done," insisted Sheridon.

"Why must it always be about you?" asked Iris. "My leaving has nothing to do with you."

"Is there someone else—someone younger?" asked Sheridon.

Iris lay her head on the blue paisley pillowcase. It felt cool and welcoming. She turned her back to him. "Don't be ridiculous."

"You don't have to leave to attend the university. You can enroll in a university in London or Paris, if you like. I'll make all of the arrangements," ameliorated Sheridon.

"I want to remain in New York," said Iris.

"Why?" asked an irritated Sheridon. "You have no family in New York, and if you leave, you will not have any source of employment."

"I will find employment," said Iris.

"Where, in someone else's house? I won't allow it. Is it money? I'll increase your salary."

"I do not want an increase in salary, and I do not want to remain in your employ. I want to be free to live my life as I please," said Iris.

"Will you at least turn around and look at me while I'm speaking to you?" asked Sheridon. Iris sighed and turned to face her employer.

"My family needs you," said Sheridon. "I want Guy to return to England with us. If you go, the entire house will be in a state of disarray. You will not leave us."

Iris turned away from him again. "My dear Sheridon, do you not realize that I have already gone?" Iris covered her head with the paisley sheet and ended all conversation with the illustrious

Sheridon Southgate. Dear Reader, I needn't tell you that a man in Sheridon Southgate's position does not take rejection lightly. Such rejection oftentimes makes a man bitter and vengeful.

• • •

Iris left the admissions office baffled. How could such a mistake have been made? She stared at the paper in her hand. The words *balance due* stood out like an emergency flare on a darkened highway. The financial aid was supposed to cover all of her expenses, but it would only cover tuition and fees. There were so many new fees added to the bill, and her attempts to obtain campus housing were unsuccessful. Where would she live? How would she support herself? It was stipulated that she could not work, apart from the meager pittance offered through the work study program. That would not be enough to afford suitable housing in New York. Iris sat in a white wrought iron chair in the outdoor seating area near the admissions office. How could this happen? She watched the summer school students go about their day smiling and laughing with canvas bags transporting laptops hanging from their shoulders. If only her life were as carefree. She would be forced to ask the Southgates for help. Iris regretted her arrogant stance with Sheridon. Now, she would have to return to him like a wounded dog asking for mercy. Perhaps Kate would be able to convince him to extend a small loan to enable her to start the fall semester. She would repay them as soon as possible. It would be a small pittance compared to Sheridon's massive fortune. But, Dear Reader, Iris's plan fails to take into consideration Sheridon's massive ego and need to control. If anyone is hoping for a positive outcome in this scenario, I admire his or her optimism. Perhaps I can interest you in the purchase of a bridge in Brooklyn

Chapter XII

All was quiet at the dinner table. Entering the dining room, Winston tried to assume a cheerful posture as he sat at the head of the table. After grace was said, Winston attempted to encourage and console his crestfallen granddaughter.

"Your grandfather is a strong man, Taylor. He'll be fine with a little rest."

Papa Sean's sudden heart attack would bring an end to Taylor's visit. The adversary had won. Papa Sean's only desire was to have Taylor by his side as he recuperated. The emerald grandfather expressed no interest in Kate's presence, and it was intimated by Grandmother Maureen that Kate's presence might actually be a detriment to the patriarch's recovery, so it was determined that Taylor would visit Papa Sean for the duration of the summer.

Courtney placed a spoonful of mashed potatoes on Guy's plate.

"I don't want any, thank you," said Guy politely.

"Yes, you will have some," said Courtney.

"Taylor doesn't have any," protested Guy pointing to his sister's barren plate.

"Taylor is excused tonight," explained Courtney.

Normally, such a remark would have elicited a mischievous grin on Taylor's face, but she sat staring blankly into her empty plate. Iris took the bowl from Courtney and placed a small portion of potatoes onto Taylor's plate. Taylor rested her head upon Iris's arm.

"You must try to eat, Taylor. It will make you strong for Papa Sean," reasoned Iris.

Taylor held onto Iris's arm. She seemed to find comfort with the gentle au pair. Iris placed a forkful of potatoes near Taylor's lips. Taylor took a small bite, still clinging to Iris's arm.

"Is Taylor going to Ireland, Grandpa?" asked Guy sensing his sister's vulnerability.

"For a short while, but she will return. Taylor will finish her vacation with us when she returns, right, Taylor?" asked Winston trying not to display any signs of disconcertion.

Taylor nodded without speaking or smiling. Her face was a cheerless rain cloud.

"When is my daddy coming home?" asked Taylor softly.

"He should be arriving tomorrow in time to take you and Iris to the airport," said Courtney tenderly. "You'll feel better when he gets here."

"I know I will," said Guy emphatically. Taylor's use of the phrase, *my daddy* stirred irritation within his heart. "I'm going to England with Daddy," blurted out the jealous youth.

Winston's heart chilled. "What are you talking about, Guy?" asked Winston with annoyance.

"Daddy said that he's taking me back to England with him, and I get to have my own room." Guy emphasized the latter part for Taylor's benefit. Sharing his room with her had been intolerable. At his new home in England, there would be room to distance himself from his annoying sister, but most importantly, he would have an opportunity to be with his father every day.

"Nothing has been decided," said Winston anxiously. He was beginning to realize the cost of competing with his son. Perhaps he could add an additional room onto the comfortable bungalow.

Guy's voice became shrill. "Yes, it has! Daddy said that I'm going with him. I'll be with him while Taylor is with her Papa Sean. It will just be the two of us."

Winston removed his napkin from his lap and placed it onto the table. He looked at Courtney.

"Finish your dinner, Guy," said Courtney gently. "We'll sort it out later."

"After we go to England, Daddy's taking me to Paris to see my mother," announced Guy innocently taking another bite of the Virginia ham.

Winston stared blankly at the loquacious youth devouring his meal nonchalantly. He turned his focus to his sister. Courtney shrugged her shoulders. It was the first time she had heard of a visit to Paris to see Guy's mother. They had never discussed Guy's mother with him; they knew little about her, apart from the fact that she was an artist and a Parisian. They knew that she wrapped Guy in a checkered tablecloth and placed him in a picnic basket with a bottle of wine and a hunk of Edam cheese on Sheridon's doorstep as an infant. As far as they were concerned, they knew all they wanted to know about Guy's mother and dreaded the thought that he would spend any time with her, particularly in Paris. Winston's greatest fear was manifesting itself. Guy was leaving him and emerging into the *world citizen* required of Sheridon Southgate's offspring.

• • •

Resting upon Iris's lap and clinging to the au pair's sleeve, Taylor held Paddy, the worn teddy bear, tightly as the Aerlingus plane ascended effortlessly through the clouds. Iris covered her fatigued charge with an airline blanket and reclined her seat as she waited for the in-flight movie. Curiously, two weeks in the United States had a negative impact upon her insatiable appetite for reading. For the past two weeks, intoxicating television consumed most of her meager leisure time. Iris consoled herself that she was not to blame for the mind-numbing television routine. Kate enjoyed American sitcoms and soap operas, and Iris found herself immersed in the plots and storylines. That would change soon. As a full-time college student, she would not have time for such frivolous diversions. Taylor drifted off into a tenuous sleep. Iris liked to watch Taylor sleep.

When Taylor was three weeks old, Iris rocked her in a tremendous antique rocking chair that Sheridon acquired for the purpose of nursing, but Taylor rejected Kate's breast milk and refused to nurse. The infant seemed happy and content when Iris rocked her in the massive chair and placed the bottle's nipple gently to her lips. Iris and Taylor bonded in the wee-small hours of the morning, as Kate nestled with Sheridon on his infrequent trips home. Ironically, the closer Kate nestled to Sheridon, the farther removed he became, and by some magnetic force, he seemed to pull the young infant with him. Taylor reveled in her father's embrace, even though the embraces were few and far between. The Southgate home was strange, indeed. Iris could not phantom how a child could be so distanced from her mother, particularly at such a young age. Predictably, Sheridon did not find the situation unusual. He expected to be loved in excess and was never disappointed. Iris imagined a huge stop sign, a technique she acquired from one of the self-help speakers Kate enjoyed watching. Enough thoughts about the Southgates; it was time to forge new vistas of brighter tomorrows.

Sheridon and Kate graciously presented Iris with a fortnight's vacation and a round-trip ticket to visit her family in the Caribbean before the start of the fall semester. She wondered what changes her sister, Peony, had made to the daintily furnished room they once shared. Iris had not seen her family in four years. Peony would be sixteen now, and her brother, Randal, would be entering manhood. Thoughts of the tranquil little island made her hunger for the sights and sounds of the marketplace and the floral aroma of the air. Everyone would marvel at her clothing and the loss of most of her accent. A local girl preparing for a medical career at a university in New York would be big news. Iris's thoughts returned to Sheridon. She did not expect her employer to relinquish control of her so easily, but she would accept the Southgate's generous donation to her educational endeavors and the trip to visit her family as a token of their appreciation for her faithful service and for agreeing to escort Taylor to Dublin. If there were strings attached, Iris did not wish to contemplate them. She would rather envision herself in a dormitory room sitting amidst a cluster of giggling girls in their nighties talking about their prospective dates. Iris imagined herself in class taking notes as a gray-haired professor droned on about microbiology. In two weeks, Iris would leave her family in the Caribbean, return to Dublin, and accompany Taylor to New York, at which time she would be free of the Southgates and ready to begin her life as an NYU freshman.

●   ●   ●

Papa Sean was too weak to meet the airplane; a distant cousin, Connor, was sent to dispatch Taylor and Iris. Sheridon would have balked at the knowledge that Taylor and Iris were transported to Papa Sean's in a common bus. Connor wore the obligatory attire of Dublin youth - jeans and tee shirt. His face was a perpetual snarl with an extended cigarette that never seemed to extinguish. The smoke irritated Iris's eyes, but she dared not express disapproval. Clearly, Connor had better things to do than escort a distant cousin and foreigner. The bus soon left the spacious area surrounding the airport and entered the congested city.

Dublin was a far-cry from New York. The people on the bus seemed remarkably simple in comparison to the well-toned commuters in New York. Iris looked out of the window and reflected upon the two cities. Pedestrians in both cities walked with determined gaits, but the eyes of the New Yorkers were unisex lasers critiquing everything that moved. Lines of gender demarcation were marked clearly in Dublin. The women's eyes were dull and lack-luster; the men's eyes were fierce, angry, and ready to fight—a call-to-arms, as it were, for any cause that presented itself. The tired bus entered the Mountjoy section. Ironically, if there was joy in the Mountjoy section of Dublin, it was not reflected in the faces of its citizens. It was a hard, gray part of town that housed a prison and seemed cloudy even on a sunny day. The attached brick houses boasted doors of festive colors. Iris wondered how such dour expressions could emerge from such brightly-colored doors. Connor walked briskly a few paces ahead and seemed annoyed at nothing in particular. At last, when he spoke, Iris was taken aback at the gentleness of his tone.

"Taylor, come here. Hold my hand," said Conner calmly. Taylor complied as blood responded to blood. Connor smiled at her and slowed his gait. Iris walked behind the pair uncomfortably. The traffic signal ticked furiously like a bomb on the brink of explosion. The sound was apropos for the area and heightened Iris's impression of Dublin as a city on the verge of eruption. Connor and Taylor stopped in front of a brick house with a cheerful, yellow door.

"Wait here," said Connor to the interloper behind him without looking back at her. Iris stood silently as Connor and Taylor entered the house. Music with throbbing rhythms eased out of the windows of one of the adjoining houses with a vibrant green door. Dark-complexioned people in foreign garb sat on the step. They did not look at Iris, and she did not look at them. A stout woman in a blue-flowered dress and a smiling, convivial face opened the door and grasped Iris's hand.

"You must be Iris. Do come inside, Dear. Connor's manners need mending."

Grandmother Maureen led Iris into the modest home and closed the effervescent yellow door quietly as Conner, a tightly-wound fuse, exited and trudged down the street.

•   •   •

Taylor's boundless energy mobilized Papa Sean. Doctors did not expect him to be able to walk outdoors for another two weeks, but the elder amazed all of his physicians. Taylor Southgate was all the medicine that Papa Sean needed. His resplendent smile greeted neighbors and friends; they remarked that his convalescence was expeditious.

For Taylor, the summer was like any other. She spent her days and nights in the company of her favorite grandfather and listened to his stories of mythological Irish heroes. The annual tradition of walking to the General Post Office to visit the statue of Cuchulainn would be observed. Grandmother Maureen walked behind the pair monitoring her husband's gait, which was surprisingly steady. The majestic, bronze statue of Cuchulainn stood behind a pane of glass within the General Post Office and inspired all passersby. Cuchulainn was such a fierce warrior that when he was mortally wounded in battle, he tied himself upright to a rock, sword and armor in hand, so that he would die standing. His enemies were so terrified of him that they dared not advance until a crow landed upon his shoulder signaling his demise. Cuchulainn, roped off by red-velvet ropes, stood as a testament to the valor of all warriors in the fight for Irish independence. Papa Sean knew that all was well now that

Taylor stood beside him before the pane. They both peered in at Cuchulainn. The heroes of Ireland were larger than life, and the annual trek to visit Cuchulainn would ensure that Taylor would never forget her glorious heritage.

•   •   •

The warm, tropical air brought a feeling of well-being to Iris as she waited for a ride to her family's home in the Caribbean.

"Iris, over here," called a tall, lanky young man in jeans and a crisp, blue shirt. The young man wore no shoes. He stood beside a green SUV. Iris approached the smiling young man.

"Randal!" she gasped. "I cannot believe it is you."

"It is good to see you," said Randal hugging his sister and placing her small bag into the SUV.

"My goodness, you are a man," said Iris agog.

"And you are quite the lady," said Randal helping his sister into the SUV.

"Randal, where did you get this vehicle? You're not involved in anything illegal, are you?" asked Iris.

Randal laughed. "Perish the thought. I am an upstanding man in this village, and our family is respected. Many things have changed since you left, Iris. Mother is supervisor of the domestic staff at the American hotel. Father suffered an accident while working on a construction site. He does not work anymore, but mother's income provides for us adequately."

"No one told me that Father had been injured," said Iris.

"Do not fear; he is well, and mother's income provides for us," said Randal driving with utmost caution.

"Does Mother earn enough for this vehicle?" asked Iris in amazement.

Randal laughed again. His laughter made Iris tense. "This is nothing," said Randal. "You must see our house. There have been many changes. Father supervised the renovations. You have your own room now, Iris. I have a recording studio where I work on my music."

"Your music?"

"I am famous for my music, Iris. I travel to many of the islands and perform at clubs and festivals. Perhaps you have heard of my group—*Ripe Melon*? Randal sang a few bars of his popular song. "I write my own music. Do you remember Avery and Clark? They accompany me on the drums and guitar. We are well-known on these islands, Iris."

"This is all very unsettling, Randal. Surely, you are not earning enough for renovations to the house, recording studios, and this type of extravagance," said Iris patting the white leather seats of the SUV.

"My group is just beginning, but after I complete my training in Seattle, Washington, I will return and become even more illustrious."

"What training? Are you training to become a singer?"

"I *am* a singer already, Iris" said Randal indignantly. "I will call Avery and Clark when we arrive home, and we will play for you. You will be proud of your brother, more so than Mother. She dismisses my singing career as frivolous nonsense and insists that I train for a position in hotel management in Seattle, Washington."

"Seattle, Washington? I don't understand any of this," said Iris bewildered.

"We have you to thank for our new position in life and our new opportunities, Iris. That wonderful saint, Mr. Sheridon Southgate, takes good care of our family, thanks to you, Iris. You are doing a fine job taking care of his wife and child. Sheridon Southgate shows his appreciation by helping us. I will be training for a management position in one of his fine American hotels, and Peony will care for his family when you begin your studies at the university. Yes, we know all about it, and we are very proud of you, Iris. The entire village is proud of you."

Iris's body began to quiver. "What do you mean Sheridon is helping you? I don't understand. How will Peony work for him? She hasn't even finished school yet."

"It is all because of the fine job that you are doing taking care of his wife and child." Randal caressed the steering wheel as if it were a precious child. "Next year this time, everyone will shed tears of joy for me, the manager of an American hotel and a famous singer. You will begin your university career, and Peony will care for the Southgate family. It has been arranged." The SUV left the paved road and turned onto the dirt road leading home. "I don't blame you for crying," consoled Randal acknowledging the tears that were beginning to stream down his sister's cheeks. "We owe it all to you, Iris, and the fine job you are doing taking care of that saint, Sheridon Southgate, and his wonderful family. The warm, tropical air seemed oppressive as Iris closed her eyes and tried to erase images of Sheridon Southgate with a halo over his head.

•   •   •

The sun glittered brightly through the hotel's terrace doors. Sheridon Southgate entered the living room and flung his cream-colored suit jacket across an easy chair. A young girl sat at his desk playing on his computer. A maid dressed in a gray uniform with a white apron and thick-soled black shoes emerged from the bathroom with a cleaning cart filled with fluffy, white towels. The maid gasped and hastened to the desk. She pulled the young girl from the desk. She bowed slightly with tears beginning to stream down her cheeks. "I am sorry, Sir. My daughter does not listen to her mother. She was supposed to tidy the desk and not handle any of your belongings. I am sorry. Please do not report me."

The woman stood with head bowed, while the young girl stood barefoot and defiant in a white smock that revealed a slender, unformed figure. Two long, silken caramel braids bedecked her face, and curious, emerald eyes sparkled at the stranger.

"Please, do not report me, Sir," pleaded the maid.

"Your daughter is rather young to be tidying the room, isn't she? Does management permit children to labor in the hotel?"

"They do not know that she helps me. My daughter is willful. She does not listen to anyone, and I cannot trust her to remain at home. Please, Sir, do not report me. I will be released if management knows that Peony is here."

Sheridon sat at the desk and examined the twosome carefully.

"Have you no husband?"

"My husband travels wherever he can find work."

"Peony, like the flower," said Sheridon thoughtfully, "lovely."

"You will not report me to management, Sir?"

"I *am* management. My name in Sheridon Southgate, and I just purchased this hotel," said Sheridon firmly. "Henceforth, there will be no children assisting with the chores of the domestic staff. Any further violations, and you will be dismissed. Am I understood?"

"Yes, Sir. Thank you, Sir. It won't happen again." The maid grabbed her daughter's hand and started for the door.

"Just a minute," said Sheridon in an authoritative voice.

The maid trembled and turned fearfully. "Yes, Sir?" asked the maid..

"Remove the cart," instructed Sheridon.

"Oh, yes, of course." The maid hastened to the towel cart and followed Peony out of the door.

"Close the door and have Peony wait outside," said Sheridon in a strange tone.

Peony looked back at her mother fearfully as the maid closed the door.

Her head was bowed low. She began to unbutton her uniform.

"What are you doing, you foolish woman. Button your dress and sit down." Sheridon pointed to the sofa near the terrace door. "I have no interest in you. My interest is in your daughter."

The maid stood quickly. "Oh, please, Sir. Peony is only twelve-years-old. She has never known a man, and she is promised."

"Promised at twelve? To whom?" asked Sheridon incredulously.

"There is a man in my village whose wife is barren. He will pay me four chickens and a goat if Peony bears a child for them."

Sheridon shuddered in disgust. "What kind of mother sells her daughter for four chickens and a goat?"

"We are poor people, Sir. Our lives are very hard on this island."

"Sit down," demanded Sheridon. "What kind of primitive civilization is this? Peony will not be sold. Am I understood?"

The woman nodded her head. "Yes, Sir," said the maid humbly.

"My new head of the domestic staff must carry herself with dignity."

The woman looked up at Sheridon in utter amazement. "Your new head of domestic staff?" asked the awe-struck maid.

"In addition," continued Sheridon, " I am here to interview for an au pair to care for my invalid wife in England. We are expecting a child next month."

The woman's face brightened. She stood eagerly. "My daughter, Iris, will work for you, Sir."

"I want Peony," said Sheridon in a dismissive tone.

"Peony is an impetuous young girl, Sir," explained the maid, "She will not be able to care for an invalid and an infant. Peony is inexperienced and will cause much grief in your house. Iris is sensible and mature. She is sixteen and has completed her schooling here. If she goes to England, she will have an opportunity to study and become a doctor. Oh, please, Sir. You will not regret selecting Iris."

Sheridon walked to the terrace doors and looked out at the crystalline ocean. "Perhaps I will accept Iris on the condition that when Peony is of age, she will replace her sister."

"Oh, thank you, Sir," said the woman joyously. Tears of joy streamed down her cheeks. "You will not regret your decision."

"I haven't decided anything yet. Bring the other girl here tomorrow at noon, and I'll have a look at her."

"Iris is pretty, Sir, and she is very smart. You will want someone smart to help with your wife and child. I am sure that you will be pleased. I will bring Iris here tomorrow at noon. Thank you Sir, thank you very much." The maid bowed several times and headed for the door.

"Don't thank me yet," admonished Sheridon.

The maid started for the door. She turned quickly. "Sir, what about Randal?"

"Who on earth is Randal?" asked Sheridon with irritation.

"Randal is my son. He and Peony are twins, and he loves to make music. Randal is eager to learn, Sir. He can be a help to you, perhaps here in this new hotel."

Sheridon considered a moment. "Bring the girl and the boy here tomorrow, and I will see what I can do for them. I warn you, if Peony is to replace her sister, her virtue must remain intact."

"I will see to it," said the anxious mother.

"Meanwhile, bring Peony back in. I would like a picture of her to show to my wife." Sheridon produced a camera from his briefcase.

"Yes, Sir," said the maid hurrying to the door. She led Peony in. Peony stood erect looking at her mother fearfully.

"Do not be afraid," said her mother impatiently. "This nice man is going to take care of us. Go and sit on his lap. I will take a picture for his wife. Go ahead now, do as I say."

Peony walked apprehensively towards Sheridon. He reached for her trembling hands and placed her on his lap. "Don't be afraid," said Sheridon softly. "You won't have to fear anything again. I promise you." The maid snapped the picture joyously.

Chapter XIII

Arnold grasped the last of the suitcases and placed them into the bluish-gray Volvo. "There," said Arnold opening the door for his granddaughter, "that's the last of them. I thought that you would have more luggage. It seems as though you have less than when you left."

"Where are Mom and Dad? I thought that they would meet me. Are they still mad?" asked Sara.

"I wanted to be the first one to see you and find out how your trip went. You didn't write or call often enough, Sara. We were worried."

"I'm sorry, Grandfather," said Sara. "Everything was so fantastic, we didn't have time to write or call. You wouldn't believe all of the things I saw. There were people shooting animals. They shot them, skinned them, and gathered around to take their meat. It was horrible, Grandfather."

"Some people live differently, Sara. Tell me about some of the fun things."

"I smoked cigarettes and drank bourbon, but please don't tell Mom and Dad. They'll kill me."

"Those aren't habits I'd like to see you develop, Sara," said Arnold nervously.

"I just wanted to try it. Everyone was smoking and drinking. That's what we did when we returned to the lodge at night."

Arnold tried to remain calm. "I hope the period of experimentation is over," said Arnold maneuvering in the traffic from Newark Airport.

"It is, Grandfather. Say, what have you been up to while I've been gone? When is Jonathan coming home again?"

"Your brother is still here. He's sharing an apartment with the young man we hired as an intern."

"Lawrence, isn't it? Funny, I didn't think that he would be Jonathan's type. He seems serious and stuffy. He's not like the others Jon hooks up with."

"*Hooks up with*? That isn't the vernacular a young woman preparing for college should be using."

Sara laughed. "How do you think college students talk, Grandfather? Oh yes, *Get thee to a nunnery*," mocked Sara. "Lighten up, Grandfather. I know what is expected of me, and I will perform admirably."

"Perform?" asked Arnold. "It isn't a performance, Sara. Your education is very important. You must speak properly if you intend to attract the appropriate sort of friends and acquaintances."

"Don't worry, Grandfather," assured Sara. "I know what to do." She took a package of cigarettes from her purse.

"I thought that you were not going to do that anymore," said Arnold.

Sara lit the cigarette and leaned her head against the headrest. "Just one more before I get home; I promise that I'll throw them away when I get home." Sara inhaled and lowered the window to release the smoke.

"I don't like this, Sara," said Arnold.

"It's the last one, Grandfather, I promise." Sara's look of enjoyment as she caressed the cigarette and inhaled the poison into her system gave Arnold pause. Perhaps the trip had been a mistake. What other vices had the ingénue acquired while soaking up culture on the African safari?

"I'm going to hold you to that promise, Sara. Don't disappoint me," said Arnold.

"Have I ever disappointed you, Grandfather? Have I ever broken my word to you?"

"No, I must admit that you haven't," said Arnold.

"And I won't now. Wait until you see what I bought you, Grandfather. I'm having it shipped home. Say, where are we going? Why are we going into the city?" asked Sara as the Volvo entered the lane for the Holland Tunnel.

"I want to check on something at the office. You don't mind if we stop for a few minutes, do you?" asked Arnold.

"Can't someone else do it, Grandfather? I'm tired. Can't we just go home? Why can't the intern do it? Isn't that what interns do? It'll take forever to get to your office in this traffic. I'm supposed to meet everyone this evening at six o'clock."

"Everyone, I take it, means the others on the safari?"

"Yes, we're going to a club in Soho."

"I will not allow you to patronize a club," said Arnold adamantly.

"Grandfather, I have *patronized* clubs before," laughed Sara. She rummaged through her purse and produced a fake ID card. Her eyes twinkled mischievously. "See? I am Sheila Glenn, and I am twenty-one years old."

Arnold shuddered. He tried to keep his eyes on the traffic, but his peripheral vision beheld a young woman clenching a cigarette between her teeth, sitting with her legs crossed at the knee rather than the ankles, and holding a fraudulent identification card. They drove in silence through the Holland Tunnel and down Broadway to lower Manhattan. Arnold pulled into a parking space that availed itself.

"Get out of the car," said Arnold.

"Can't I wait here, Grandfather? I'm tired."

"We will walk to the office. I want to talk to you."

Sara opened the ashtray and extinguished the cigarette. "All right, Grandfather. No more cigarettes or fake ID. I'll just tear this up, see?" Sara ripped the identification card into pieces.

"You'll get another one," said Arnold. "Wait here." Arnold stepped out of the car and made a phone call on his cell phone. He spoke for several minutes then returned to the car. "All right, come with me."

"Where are we going?" asked Sara. "Did you tell Mom and Dad? "

"Get out of the car," said Arnold calmly.

Sara sighed heavily as she exited the Volvo. "I'm sorry, Grandfather. I promise that it won't happen again."

As they walked along the sidewalk, Arnold held his granddaughter's hand and fought images of unsupervised teenagers drinking and smoking in luxurious accommodations thousands of miles away from home.

"I thought that you would be able to handle the independence. Where were the chaperones while all of this drinking and smoking were going on?"

"We got up after they went to sleep," laughed Sara. "We wore them out during the day so that they would retire early."

"The director will hear from me this very day," asserted Arnold. Sara released his hand.

"What are you going to do? You can't tell. You'll get everyone in trouble, and they'll blame me. Please don't do anything, Grandfather."

"I cannot tell you how disappointed I am, Sara. You have really let me down."

"I'm sorry," said Sara. She reached for her grandfather's hand and held it tightly.

Arnold was unmoved. "I know that the world is a different place than when I was a youth, but certain things do not change. There are certain behaviors expected of a young lady, Sara."

"I know, Grandfather," said Sara tightening her grip on his hand.

The words were spoken with sincerity, but Arnold knew that behind them lurked a Sara that he neither knew nor trusted.

"How about some pizza?" asked Arnold as they passed a pizzeria, which claimed to serve the best pizza in New York. Sara loved pepperoni pizza.

"No thanks, Grandfather. I'm not hungry." Sara's eyes rested on the liquor store sign hanging adjacent to the pizzeria. "I'm not hungry at all. Did you call Mom and Dad? Will they be waiting for me at the office?

"Why would you think that, Sheila?" asked Arnold.

"You watched me rip up the false ID, and I promised that I would stop drinking and smoking. They won't understand, Grandfather. They're not like you."

"I don't understand either, Sara. Why would you behave this way?" asked Arnold.

"I get stressed sometimes," said Sara wishing that she had a cigarette to calm the mounting tension she felt. Her heart began to pound against her chest. "They'll ground me for the entire summer. I'll be trapped in my room for the entire summer. You didn't call them, did you, Grandfather?"

Arnold remained silent. Sara averted her eyes from a sign advertising wine and spirits. She thought of the calmness she always experienced with a drink slowly making its way through her system. First, her hands would feel lax, then, her feet would begin to tingle. Her body would dismiss all tension and embrace a gratifying stillness. Perhaps keeping her promise would not be as easy as she thought.

• • •

The World Trade Center Plaza was festive. Workmen set up the stage and placed white aluminum chairs in neat rows for the afternoon concert. The seats filled quickly as people gathered in the concert area.

"Here, let's sit down for awhile," said Arnold. He directed Sara to an empty chair. "I want to discuss something with you."

"Grandfather, I've been sitting on a plane all night, and I'm exhausted. If you called Mom and Dad to take me home, I'd rather just sit here quietly and wait for the fireworks."

"If I thought that calling your parents would help, I would call them. They're preoccupied with the new house and won't give this matter the attention it deserves. I have another suggestion. I need you to help me get things running smoothly upstairs in the new offices."

"What new offices?" asked Sara.

"Your brother and Lawrence are working on a summer initiative program for inner-city students."

"And you want *me* to help?" laughed Sara. "I don't know what kind of help I would be, Grandfather. The inner-city is not exactly my milieu." Sara wished that she had a cigarette between her fingers. She imagined the feel of it and the aroma of the intoxicating smoke.

Arnold smiled. "Well, at least you are beginning to speak like my granddaughter. Your role would be that of an assistant to Jonathan and Lawrence. You can help with the paper work."

"Wow, that sounds exciting!" mocked Sara.

"Since you're free for the rest of the summer, I thought that you might want to help. Besides, it would give me an opportunity to see you."

"To monitor me," corrected Sara.

"You're good with computers," said Arnold.

"Jonathan and Lawrence don't need me," said Sara. "Besides, I have plans for the summer. It's the last chance I have to spend time with my friends before we go to college. I don't know when I'll see them again. I suppose that's your plan."

"The position enables you to reside in one of the corporate apartments for the summer."

Sara grasped her grandfather's arm. Her eyes beamed. "Do you mean that I can have my own apartment?"

"You will share the apartment with Jonathan."

"Oh, now I get it," said Sara. "You're placing me under twenty-four hour surveillance. I'll be here in the office all day and with Jonathan all night."

"Let's go upstairs and tell your brother the good news," said Arnold.

The overhead television monitors were tuned to CNN. The sounds of ringing telephones, chatty keyboards, and cheerful conversation blended with the sound of buzz saws and hammers reconfiguring the offices. Gone was the elegant conference room. In its stead was what seemed to be a greenhouse. The office was staffed with young people dressed in jeans and khakis. No one appeared to be over twenty-five.

"What is all of this, Grandfather?" asked Sara looking around.

"I'm beginning to wonder the same thing," said Arnold looking into the greenhouse. Tall, lush tropical plants brushed against the ceiling of the greenhouse; the air was humid.

"This might be fun after all," laughed Sara.

They proceeded to a nearby office. The overhead television monitor was tuned to the nature channel, and the music of Bach played softly in the background. Jonathan sat comfortably in an amber leather swivel chair behind a mahogany desk. An endless array of books filled mahogany bookshelves, which encircled the room. A brown, long-haired dachshund stretched out on an Oriental rug. The resplendent view of the New York skyline posed within the panoramic window. Brocade drapes hung from floor to ceiling. The dog stood on its short legs and focused its attention on the two visitors. Its bark was friendly, and it began to sniff Arnold and Sara's ankles.

"Jonathan, what is all of this?" asked Arnold moving towards the desk.

Jonathan, playing his cello softly, stood smiling. "Sara, you're back." He leaned the cello against the desk and hugged his sister.

"Why is there a dog in the office?" asked Arnold.

"Not just any dog, Grandfather. This is Freemont. Stephen and I picked him up in New Hampshire last weekend." Jonathan held the dog up for the necessary introductions.

"You went to New Hampshire? I left you and Lawrence in charge. You can't go traipsing off to New Hampshire on weekends, especially now that your sister is going to be helping you."

"Oh yes," said Jonathan, "the new job. Well, Sara, I hope that you will find the office to your liking. You'll have quite a bit of responsibility here and at home. Think you can handle it?"

"Do I have a choice?" Sara picked Freemont up. He licked her forehead.

"We need to talk," said Arnold tensely. "Get the dog out of here."

"Freemont, Grandfather. His name is Freemont," said Jonathan.

"Look at my face, Jonathan," said Arnold. "Do I seem amused?"

"No, Sir, you do not look amused." Jonathan used the military "Sir" when his grandfather became overbearing.

"Come on, Freemont," said Sara. "I think this conversation will be about us." Sara led Freemont into the outer offices.

"You look flabbergasted, Grandfather," observed Arnold.

"I wasn't expecting a dog and a greenhouse," said Arnold. "These are offices, Jonathan, they should look and function as offices."

"Stephen and I thought that the greenhouse would be the perfect backdrop for our environmental programs."

"What environmental programs, and where is Lawrence?" asked Arnold impatiently.

"Stephen is having lunch with one of the contributors to the Computers-in-Schools Program," said Jonathan. "The programs are up and running, Grandfather. Stephen will give you a full report when he returns."

"I would like a report on that greenhouse. Just how much is it costing me?"

"It isn't costing the corporation anything, Grandfather. The environmental agency that we teamed with provided it free of charge. It's a new experimental program that tests the effects of a greenhouse within the working environment. We have been able to entice many botany students to spend the summer volunteering to work with the program. I might add that the greenhouse is tax deductible. I told you that I would not let you down, Grandfather. Everything is running smoothly."

"Things are not running smoothly. Your sister has a drinking problem, and it didn't start with that safari. She has a fraudulent identification card, and she has been frequenting clubs that serve alcohol for quite some time. Your parents cannot control her."

"And you think that I will have greater success?"

"You'd better if you want these summer programs to continue. Give your sister something to do that will keep her busy. I don't want her out of your sight. Why is your hand trembling?" asked Arnold.

Jonathan held his tremulous hand. "Just a little twitch," said Jonathan. "I've been preparing for my chamber music group's summer concert at the MET. I suppose I've been overworking my hands. You must attend, Grandfather."

"Tell Simmons to put it on my schedule, and get Dr. Goldberg to check that hand," said Arnold. "Is everything ready at the apartment?"

"Don't worry, Sara is in good hands," assured Jonathan. "How will you convince Mom and Dad to allow her to stay in the city?"

"You will convince them that you need her help with these programs and can collaborate effectively if you work together at work and at home. I don't want those morons anywhere near Sara. They must have known about the visits to these clubs. It doesn't take a brain surgeon to figure out that she would need false ID in order to get in. Your parents dropped the ball, but I won't. I want a full report each day."

"I won't disappoint you," said Jonathan.

"And make an appointment to get that hand checked. I don't like the looks of it," said Arnold exiting the genteel office.

"Will do," said Jonathan. He returned to his desk as the tremors in his hand increased. With his steady hand, he placed a capsule into his mouth and waited for the tremors to subside.

Chapter XIV

Sara surveyed her new apartment and found that the décor was not open for debate. As always, Jonathan, the most territorial human being she had ever encountered, had placed his mark, so to speak, upon everything. Accustomed to her brother's obsessive preoccupation with art and antiques, Sara reasoned that she would learn to tolerate the exquisite Thomas Eakin prints that graced the living room walls in exchange for privacy and freedom from parental bondage. Slowly and deliberately moving through the apartment with Freemont sniffing her footsteps, Sara felt both relieved and anxious. Freemont's long, shiny brown hair whisked the pale blue carpet as he walked on his short, stubby legs.

"What's this?" asked Sara picking up a small prescription container. Jonathan snatched it from her hand in a manner that was most unlike his calm, easy-going manner.

"I'll take that," said Jonathan placing the container in his pocket.

"What are all of these plants?" asked Sara. "You have a greenhouse at the office, and the apartment looks like a rain forest. Since when did you become so interested in horticulture?"

Several tall tropical plants graced the apartment. They seemed out of place and eager to find a spacious home that would permit them to unfold their hidden beauty.

"I'm keeping them for a friend," responded Jonathan curtly. "They will be placed in the greenhouse."

"Why is there a greenhouse in the office? I don't understand why Grandfather allowed you to get away with that one."

"Don't annoy me with foolish questions, Sara. There is rhyme and reason for everything I do," retorted Jonathan. " This will be your room. I expect you to keep it clean. That should be challenge enough for you."

Jonathan opened the door to a spacious, airy bedroom filled with bright, glowing sunbeams. A blue-striped comforter covered the queen-sized bed. Crisp, white curtains adorned the windows. A small, white French provincial desk with gold trim brightened a corner near the window. Sunbeams streamed into the room and provided a festive ambiance. The cheerful room was filled with books on tall, white shelves with gentle flowering plants peeking over ledges.

"I purchased the desk for you today. I suppose you will need a vanity of some sort. I ordered one from my antique dealer. With any luck, it should arrive tomorrow morning," said Jonathan brushing dog hair from the comforter. "Freemont adores this room." The sun bathed Freemont's elongated body as he stretched out on the comforter and closed his eyes for a nap.

"Don't go to any trouble on my account. Sorry to put you out, Freemont," said Sara. "I don't plan spend much time in the apartment."

"We'll discuss that after you get settled. I am not anticipating any problems with drinking or smoking, Sara. They are both prohibited here. You do understand that, don't you?"

"Fear not. I intend to mend my wicked ways and become the perfect house guest."

"Good. You should know that Grandfather can be brutal in matters of this sort. You can unpack. We'll be having dinner with Stephen later."

"You and Grandfather are too kind. I am without words—simply speechless," said Sara opening her suitcase on the bed.

"Don't be flippant. We are working on your behalf. A little gratitude would be appropriate," said Jonathan.

Sara bowed humbly. "Thank you ever so much. I have one request."

"What is it?" asked Jonathan impatiently.

"If I must have paintings on the walls, may I select the paintings?"

Jonathan's face clouded. "What did you have in mind?"

"I don't know," said Sara with a sigh. "Everyone is not enamoured with Monet. You're surrounding me with paintings of flowers because I'm a female—rather stereotypical, don't you think?"

Jonathan was taken aback. "The paintings were not selected for you."

Sara grinned mischievously. "Don't tell me that you purchased these paintings for that Lawrence guy."

"Stephen appreciates my taste in art," said Jonathan indignantly. "I plan to hang them in his office when you move into the dormitory."

Sara's grin emerged into a laugh. "Jonathan, I hate to be the bearer of bad news, but Lawrence is not the kind of guy who likes flowers or paintings of flowers."

"Upon what are you basing your analysis?"

"Instinct, my dear brother. Lawrence is a visitor to your little *community*. Don't expect him to take up permanent residence. It won't happen. Anyway, I'm more his type. If he had one scintilla of personality, I might be interested, strictly on a summer basis, mind you," said Sara confidently.

Jonathan smirked. "Thank you for the analysis, but you should concentrate your energies on preparing the room to suit your taste, your budding, decadent taste. If you insist upon hanging posters of pea-brained guitarists with earrings stapled into their lips, please have the common decency to keep the door closed."

"I will," said Sara closing the door as her brother exited. She took a small bottle of bourbon out of the suitcase and fingered it tenderly. Freemont opened his eyes and watched Sara hide the bottle in her closet.

•   •   •

At dusk, Sara heard a gentle knock on the door. "Sara, open the door. We're going out for dinner," announced Jonathan.

Sara opened the door in an oversized, white terrycloth bathrobe and flip flops. "You two go ahead. I want to tackle the freshman summer reading list."

Jonathan looked at his sister with incredulity.

"I do read from time to time," said Sara producing a rather thick copy of *Paradise Lost* with commentary. "Go ahead. I'll be fine."

"I think that you should come with us," said Jonathan warily. It was quite unlike his sister to prepare for bed before midnight, and the prospect of her reading Milton voluntarily was unfathomable, to say the least.

"I know that you don't trust me, but where can I go? The doorman watches my every move. I'm certain that he will alert you if I try to leave. You don't have any cigarettes or alcohol in the apartment, and I certainly don't have any. Would you like to frisk me or smell my breath?" asked Sara. Freemont barked.

"All right, but I'll be ten minutes away," warned Jonathan. "If you break your promise, Sara, I can assure you that the consequences will be dire."

"I will not break my promise. Go ahead, you two. I'll be fine."

Jonathan and Stephen exited the apartment. Freemont snuggled next to Sara on their bed as she read her book.

"You should not have left her alone," said Stephen as they exited the building.

"Hello, Thornton," said Jonathan acknowledging the doorman.

"May I get a cab for you, Mr. Cohen?" asked the smiling doorman.

"No thanks, Thornton, we'll walk," said Jonathan. Stephen neither spoke nor looked at the gregarious doorman. The twosome walked slowly in the warm evening air.

"I don't think that I can get used to this," said Stephen. "He's always there."

"Do you not like Thornton?" asked Jonathan.

"We never have any privacy; his presence is intrusive. The man watches everything and everyone," complained Stephen.

Jonathan smiled. "Precisely. These are the corporate apartments, Stephen. Yes, there is a loss of privacy, but the Thornton's of the world safeguard properties of this sort. Thornton can repel unwelcome guests and intruders."

"I suppose," conceded Stephen.

"Speaking of privacy," said Jonathan, "how are things on the twelfth floor with Phillip? If it isn't working out, we are under no obligation to remain in the corporate apartments."

"Didn't you tell your grandfather that we would supervise your sister? Of course, we are under obligation."

"What I mean is, we can get another apartment nearby. I can check on Sara often, and, as you mentioned, Thornton is always on call."

"That's absurd," said Stephen. "Why go to all of that expense and trouble?"

"It's no trouble at all," said Jonathan reasonably.

Stephen stopped walking. "Something is wrong. What is it?"

Jonathan smiled, and they began walking again. "Sara said something curious this afternoon. She said that you were only visiting my little *community* and given the opportunity, you might be more interested in her than in me."

Stephen looked perplexed. "You're listening to Sara now? You failed to notice that she was fully clothed under that decoy robe. I noticed the cuff of her jeans extending beneath the robe. She's probably drinking herself into a stupor at this instant. I don't know why you agreed to leave her alone," said Stephen with irritation. "What did she mean by *community*?"

"It isn't important," said Jonathan. "But you're right. I failed to notice the jeans. Perhaps we should start back."

"Why not let Thornton do his job. He'll tell you if she goes out or attempts to have alcohol delivered. You searched her room, didn't you?" asked Stephen.

"Of course I didn't. Sara is not a prisoner, Stephen. I won't treat her as such. She gave her word, and I trust that she'll keep it."

Stephen shook his head sardonically. "Your parents trusted her, and she used fake ID to enter clubs in order to drink. Your grandfather trusted her, and Sara and her pals boozed up a storm on safari. If she were my sister, I would hold her accountable for her actions. Why are you holding your hand like that? Why is it trembling?" asked Stephen.

"It's nothing. I need my medication. Reach into my pocket and get one of the pills out of the container, will you?"

Stephen opened the small container and placed a tablet in Jonathan's tremulous hand. Jonathan swallowed it quickly.

"When will we discuss this, Jonathan?" asked Stephen. "You continuously deny that there is anything wrong, yet, the tremors seem to increase daily."

"All things in time," said Jonathan softly. The pill seemed to induce a rapid state of lethargy. "Let's dine here, shall we? You don't mind if we have Chinese tonight, do you?"

"You hate Chinese food."

" I'd like to sit down. I'm feeling rather tired."

A hostess led them to a table in the darkened, candlelit Chinese restaurant.

"Nothing for me," said Stephen as the waitress placed a menu before Stephen; he shoved it away.

"Please give us a moment," said Jonathan cordially. The waitress smiled and left them alone. "All right, you leave me no choice. I don't want to worry you, but I'm flying to Brazil tomorrow afternoon."

Stephen looked askance at Jonathan as he continued. "There are tropical plants that I must have, and I will make my selections tomorrow."

Stephen closed his eyes and attempted to shield his annoyance. "You are trembling like a leaf and can barely hold yourself upright. Your alcoholic sister…"

"Sara is not an alcoholic," insisted Jonathan weakly.

"Your alcoholic sister just moved in," continued Stephen, "and you are her chief caretaker; in addition, we are beginning several new summer programs, most of which you initiated, and you want to travel to Brazil to purchase plants?"

"I promise that I will share more details with you when I return. Trust me, Stephen. I will explain everything when I return. We will go to the office tomorrow morning and sort out any glitches before I leave. I assure you that it will all make sense upon my return."

"What about Sara? What if she starts drinking in your absence?"

"Sara can be trusted, and you will be there to help monitor her actions."

"I don't want to monitor Sara's actions. She should be placed in some sort of rehabilitation program, Jonathan, You and your grandfather know this."

"Two days, that is all I ask. Help me with this, and in two days, I will explain everything. All will be back to normal," said Jonathan sipping his glass of water.

Stephen watched Jonathan try to hold his hand steady

"You must see a doctor, Jonathan."

"Two days. That is all I ask. Trust me." Jonathan returned the glass to the table.

Stephen removed the wrapper from a fortune cookie. *You will find the happiness you seek soon.* Stephen tossed the cookie back into the bowl.

"Bad news?" asked Jonathan.

"The usual," said Stephen with a hope-filled heart. Two days was not an unreasonable length of time to establish a lifetime of bliss.

• • •

"Back so soon?" asked Sara upon her brother's arrival. She stretched out on the sofa sipping a bottle of sparkling water. "You look awful. What happened?"

"Nothing," said Jonathan. "I'm going to bed early. Stephen will come down and take Freemont out around ten or so." Jonathan turned abruptly. "I must say, you surprised me, Sara. We anticipated the worst." He started for his room; Freemont followed close behind. "Goodnight. I'll see you in the morning." Jonathan entered his bedroom.

"I thought that you might need this," said Sara. She placed a small piece of paper on Jonathan's nightstand. "Dr. Halpern called and said that he wants to see you as soon as possible."

"Thanks," said Jonathan placing the message in the drawer of the nightstand.

"When you want to talk about it, let me know," said Sara. "Whatever you're hiding will surface sooner or later. From your haggard appearance, I'd say that it will be sooner rather than later. You need help; I need help. We can help each other." Sara placed the miniature bottle of bourbon on Jonathan's nightstand. "I didn't drink it because you trusted me. Now I'm asking you to trust me with whatever is troubling you. Who is Dr. Halpern?"

Jonathan considered briefly. He picked up the small bottle of bourbon and looked at it intently. "Stephen said that I should search your room, but I told him that you could be trusted. Thank you for keeping your word."

"Who is Dr. Halpern?" asked Sara again.

"Dr. Halpern is the herbalist treating my condition," explained Jonathan. "I'll be flying to Brazil tomorrow afternoon."

"Condition? Brazil? Jonathan, what..."

"Something is attacking my nervous system," interrupted Jonathan, "The local doctors have offered no hope and seem to think that I may be confined to a wheelchair in two or three years."

Sara shuddered at the news.

"There is no reason for concern," assured Jonathan. "Dr. Halpern is a genius. Those plants are part of my holistic treatment. Their beauty calms my nerves, and extract from their leaves in the hands of my pharmacist produces these wonder pills. The plants aren't legal in this country. I import them from Brazil."

"Import them?"

"My sources get them past customs and bring them into the country. My body chemistry changes frequently; it is necessary to travel to Brazil to ensure that the selected plants and my current needs are compatible."

"This sounds risky, Jonathan. I think that you should tell Grandfather. He'll know what to do. What if the police discover these plants? "

"That's the least of my concerns, Sara. I fear that my body is becoming immune to the pills," said Jonathan with trepidation.

"Why must you travel all the way to Brazil? Why can't Dr. Halpern come here?"

"Dr. Halpern's experimental treatments are not actually legal in this country. If he enters the country, there will be problems, and I will lose a brilliant doctor and any hope of recovery," replied Jonathan.

"You're not thinking this through, Jonathan. There must be a reason why the treatments are not legal in this country."

"I have everything under control," assured Jonathan.

"What will you do?" asked Sara.

"I will fly to Brazil tomorrow afternoon. I don't want Mom, Dad, or Grandfather to know where I've gone."

"You're making a mistake. Please don't do this," pleaded Sara.

"I must, and I am counting on you to keep your promise and stay away from the alcohol and the cigarettes. I also expect you to assist in the offices while I'm gone. The summer initiatives programs must begin on schedule."

"Why are you worrying about those silly programs?" asked Sara.

"I want you to promise that you will take care of yourself and not create any unnecessary problems."

"I will keep my promise, and I will help you," sighed Sara.

"One more thing, Stephen must know nothing of this."

Sara frowned. "Why haven't you told him? Are you afraid that he will bolt like a frightened rabbit when he finds out that you are ill?"

"Quite the contrary," said Jonathan climbing into his bed, "I am afraid that he will remain because I am ill." He turned off the light on the nightstand indicating dismissal. Sara closed the door and exited the room quietly.

• • •

The evening air was muggy and oppressive, but not as oppressive as the air in Jonathan and Sara's corporate apartment. Stephen pressed the button for the elevator. Doormen, corporate apartments, lavish furnishings—Stephen wondered how the rich lived with themselves. His humble background from a small, nondescript New Jersey town had not prepared him for such opulence or for such characters as Jonathan and Sara Cohen. They, too, were from New Jersey, but Stephen doubted if they had ever encountered the small-town manners and lifestyle that engulfed his personality. He did not understand them, and they did not understand him. How did he become involved with these people? To them, he was an amusing diversion to pass the summer and nothing more. Jonathan's secrecy confirmed that. Running off to gather plants in Brazil when he was clearly ill was unspeakable madness; leaving at the onset of programs that he initiated was the height of negligence. Monitoring a teenaged alcoholic was a repugnant task, and Stephen marveled at the cost of privilege.

"I've come for Freemont," said Stephen dryly as Sara opened the door.

"Come in. I'll get him." Sara placed the harness over Freemont's soft, shiny hair and attached the leash. "There, he's all ready for his walk."

"I think that Freemont should remain with me and Phillip until Jonathan returns," said Stephen.

"I can take care of him," said Sara. She had grown accustomed to the little creature's warm, soft fur nestled against her as she slept.

"I doubt that," said Stephen. "I will be required to take care of both you in Jonathan's absence. It will be easier if Freemont remains with me upstairs."

"I suppose you'd like to place a harness and leash around both of us. It would make your job a lot easier, wouldn't it?" asked Sara indignantly. Stephen did not respond.

"You needn't concern yourself with me, Mr. Lawrence. I'll get Freemont's bowl and brush. I don't want to see you here until Jonathan returns."

"That sounds like a good idea," said Stephen. Sara returned with Freemont's dog food, bowl, and hair brush.

"Thank you," said Stephen.

"And don't forget this," said Sara placing a stuffed rabbit with the other items in Stephen's arms. "Freemont loves his stuffed rabbit. See the rabbit run."

"I'm certain that there is some meaning to that remark," said Stephen," but I have neither the time nor the inclination to pursue it. Good night."

Sara slammed the door. "Arrogant jerk," uttered Sara. "What Jonathan sees in you, I will never know."

"Problem?" Jonathan stood in his bedroom doorway. His blue-striped pajamas seemed oversized on his thin, pale body.

"I don't intend to work with that jerk," said Sara. "I feel like he's judging me."

"We need you to help get the programs underway, Sara. You promised that you would help."

"I will be more of a help if I stay away. If I'm forced to work with that self-righteous baboon, I *will* begin drinking."

"Do you propose to remain in the apartment all day and night? I cannot permit that," said Jonathan sitting on the sofa patiently.

"I am not a child, Jonathan, and I will not be monitored by Stephen Lawrence. He's not much older than I am, and he certainly has no authority in Cohen Enterprises. It's belittling. Can't you see that?"

"It's either Stephen or Grandfather. Perhaps you would prefer Mother or Father," said Jonathan rationally. "Now, I must get some sleep. Let me know your preference in the morning. One thing is certain; you will not remain unsupervised for the duration of my trip."

"You don't get to make that decision, Jonathan!" yelled Sara.

"Fine, then we'll let Grandfather make it." Jonathan started for his bedroom.

"Wait," said Sara familiar with her grandfather's harshness when he suspects that the family structure is endangered. "Let's compromise. I will go to the offices and assist, if Stephen does not enter this apartment. Freemont can remain with Stephen and Phillip; he will see me every day at the office to monitor my progress. He is such an acknowledged *expert*, I am certain that he will detect whether or not I have been drinking or smoking."

"Under condition that you phone and check in with him on the hour every evening," insisted Jonathan. "It's against my better judgment, but I must travel to Brazil tomorrow afternoon. I have no recourse. Perhaps you'd like Phillip to check on you."

"Phillip is creepy. I don't want him here either. I could go to Brazil with you."

"You will not go to Brazil with me," said Jonathan. "You must stay here and work with the program so that Grandfather will not become suspicious."

"You want me to lie to Grandfather? What if he asks where you are?"

"He thinks that I am practicing with my chamber music group for our performance at the MET. He'll believe that and won't expect to see me for a couple of days. I have already discussed it with him. Now all you have to do is cooperate down at the offices and here at the apartment. I will return as soon as I can. Please help me, Sara. We need each other."

"I will not check in with Stephen Lawrence. How can I phone him every hour if I am asleep?"

"Those are my conditions. You will phone in on the hour from the moment you enter the apartment, which should be around five or so, until eleven PM. Do you accept the terms?"

"Are you assuming that I cannot smoke or drink after II PM?"

"No, but at II PM the cameras will be in full operation in every room of the apartment."

"What cameras?" asked Sara timorously.

"The ones Grandfather had installed before your arrival. I told you that he can be brutal in these matters, Sara. As long as I am here, they are inoperable. The moment I leave, they will be utilized to monitor the apartment. I am extending trust by not using them during the hours I specified."

"I do not believe this. I am being monitored by cameras? This is like being in prison," said Sara incredulously. "This apartment is no better than a prison cell."

"You brought this upon yourself, Sara."

"And what about you? Doesn't Grandfather care what you and Lawrence do here in the apartment? Why are your actions off limits?" asked Sara.

"I am a man. It's different for a woman."

"What?" asked an indignant Sara.

" I don't make the rules," said Jonathan. "Now, I must go to sleep. I will see you in the morning."

Sara looked around the walls and ceilings for signs of cameras. Nothing was visible. She wondered if Jonathan fabricated the use of cameras to frighten her.

• • •

Jonathan sat at his desk working on a new composition for his cello. Nigel, his youthful assistant, entered and watered the plants on the desk carefully, so as not disturb his debonair employer. Nigel's internship for two months in New York was a dream come true. California was warm and relaxed, but New York had the finest theater experiences, and the budding thespian lived and breathed New York theater in his off-duty hours. On weekends, he worked as an usher at the Delacourt Theater in Central Park. One day, he would be the lead in one of the plays, but for now, Nigel's internship with the Cohen Enterprises Summer Initiatives Program and the completion of his studies at UC Berkeley took precedence. Jonathan placed Mitzi in her corner. Nigel placed two new books on the bookshelf and dusted the others with a pristine white cloth. Freemont wandered into the open door, sat on his pillow near the window, and watched contentedly as Nigel placed a crystal goblet and two bottles of sparkling water on coasters on the desk. The diminutive youth filled a decorative jar with pretzels and placed them next to the morning edition of the *New York Times*. Stephen entered and sat on the stuffed, burgundy leather chair alongside the desk. A café latte and carrot muffin were in place on a small end table near the chair. Jonathan perused the newspaper as Stephen settled back for the morning meeting.

"Mr. Brielle is coming today to see his office, Nigel. Is it ready?" asked Jonathan munching softly on the pretzel.

"Yes," answered Nigel. "I'll put the finishing touches on it this morning. I'm thinking of a tweed wing chair and ottoman. I'm told that he is partial to them. They should arrive around noon."

"What about the floral arrangements? Hibiscus might work with the tweed," suggested Jonathan.

"Tweed with hibiscus? Something in the ivy family would be more appropriate, I assure you," advised Nigel.

Stephen shifted in his seat impatiently. "Are we having a meeting this morning, or not? If not, there are things I can do while you two discuss floral arrangements."

"Thank you, Nigel," said Jonathan patiently nibbling a pretzel. "I trust your judgment implicitly."

Nigel nodded and closed the door.

"My, we are curt this morning," said Jonathan. "Difficult evening?"

"If you call arguing with your sister difficult, then yes, I had a difficult evening. I don't think that this monitoring is going to work, Jonathan," said Stephen.

"I have already discussed it with her. We will employ the use of the cameras from eleven p.m. to six a.m. She will phone in with you on the hour prior to eleven."

"Phone in with me?" asked Stephen bewildered. "Am I expected to be on phone duty all night? Am I being monitored as well?"

"Of course not," said Jonathan. "Sara isn't comfortable with you. I thought that the phone monitoring would be an option. It can work, Stephen. It's only for two days."

"Two days of camera and phone surveillance. When were you going to tell me about the cameras? You mean they've been in there all along?"

"They are only used in emergencies, Stephen. All of the corporate apartments have cameras. I will show you how to operate them."

Stephen sighed with discomfort. He felt as though he was sliding down a treacherous hilltop on a glazed sheet of ice, and at the bottom waited an implacable stone wall.

"You also failed to inform me about the new addition to the Computers-in-Schools program, Winston Brielle. I thought that I had full control over hiring. Who is this guy, and why wasn't I informed that he'd be working with us?" asked Stephen.

"Winston Brielle is a friend of my grandfather's. Interestingly, Winston Brielle is Sheridon Southgate's father."

Stephen sat erect in the comfortable chair. "Sheridon Southgate's father wants to work with us? That doesn't make any sense."

"As I understand it, Winston Brielle has been raising Sheridon's son. Sheridon wants to take the boy to England with him when he returns."

"Why is your grandfather involved in this matter? It's a no-win situation. Winston Brielle cannot prevent Sheridon Southgate from taking his son to England, and if the boy returns to England with his father, he will be in the clutches of pure evil," said Stephen analytically.

Jonathan searched Stephen's face. "You *are* judgmental today, aren't you?"

"I'm merely stating that a position in the summer initiatives program seems more like a comfort zone to heal the old gentleman's impending loss. What are we expected to do with him? How do you imagine he'll fit in around here?"

Jonathan poured more sparkling water into his crystal goblet and added a lime wedge. "Just keep him busy. He's a retired school principal. He can be helpful working with the students and school officials. He adds credibility to the program. Fear not, Winston Brielle will not be a burden."

"What about his salary? We have a full staff already. Where are we going to get the additional funds for this computer program? Have you any idea what it will cost?"

"That, my friend," said Jonathan," is your department. I will handle the creative end, and you will take care of the logistics. Don't worry, my grandfather will be pleased when he finds that Winston Brielle is in charge of the program and will donate the necessary funding. It's all tax deductible. "

"You're placing Brielle in charge of the program?" asked Stephen incredulously. "How do we know that he can handle this responsibility, Jonathan?"

"It doesn't matter. You're there to assist in the event that he is not up-to-par, and I will return in two days."

"Oh yes, so, you're still intent on flying to South America this afternoon to bring back a handful of tropical plants."

"Select, Stephen, I am going to select certain plants that will be suitable."

"Suitable for what?" asked Stephen perplexed.

"For me. I must be there to test them to see if I am compatible."

"You want to be compatible with a plant? Are you losing your mind?"

"I will explain everything when I return. I have a two-day grace period, remember? There will be no questions until the grace period has expired."

"My life was a lot simpler before I met you," sighed Stephen.

"Yes, but look at the person you have become since our meeting," said Jonathan.

"Yes," lamented Stephen, "Just look at what I have become. Enjoy your trip." Stephen exited the office somberly.

• • •

Winston Brielle sat behind his new desk in amazement. "I never expected anything like this."

"This is temporary, I assure you. Your wing chair and ottoman have not arrived as yet, but they will be here before the day's end," said Nigel.

"I'm overwhelmed. I don't need all of this," said Winston humbly.

"If you need anything, don't hesitate to phone," said Nigel presenting Winston with a silver cell phone. "I'm on speed dial, number three. Mr. Cohen, Arnold Cohen, is number one. He wants you to call him if you have any concerns."

"Well look at this," said Winston marveling at the small phone. "I don't think I've ever seen one so small. Just what is your function here, Nigel?"

"I am Mr. Cohen's, Jonathan, that is, personal assistant. I will assist you until Jonathan assigns someone."

"And what am I going to be doing in this marvelous office?" asked Winston.

"I have not been instructed yet, Mr. Brielle, as to the nature of your assignment. Perhaps you would like to familiarize yourself with some of our programs. I have a brochure here."

Winston leafed through the brochure. "Thank you, Nigel. I'll read this until I'm given a directive. Is Jonathan available?"

"Jonathan will be rehearsing with his chamber music group for a couple of days, but Stephen will speak with you later this afternoon."

"Stephen?"

"Stephen Lawrence runs things up here with Jonathan, and he's number two on your speed dial. Stephen's out of the office, but he's scheduled to speak with you when he returns."

"Oh, I see. Well you've been very helpful. Thank you, Nigel. You seem rather young to be an assistant. May I ask how old you are?

"I am seventeen, Sir," answered Nigel.

"Oh, still in high school, eh?"

"No, Sir. I am a sophomore at UC Berkeley. Is there anything I can get for you until Stephen arrives?"

"No, thank you, Nigel," said Winston. "I suppose it would be all right to walk around and get the feel of the place."

"Actually, Stephen wants to give you the grand tour."

"Oh, of course, I'll wait for Stephen. Thank you, Nigel."

"No problem." Nigel smiled and exited Winston's office. Winston walked to the window. Looking down at the street made him dizzy. Plants hung in wicker baskets from the ceiling and protruded gracefully from two large wicker baskets in diagonal corners of the room. A greenish-tweed sofa created the warmth of a living room. Large, olive green throw pillows adorned the sofa. They looked so inviting that Winston sat on the sofa and rested his head upon the pillows.

After a while, Winston felt a soft nudge. "Mr. Brielle, it's time to go."

Winston opened his eyes to see a tall, stalwart young man with brown, wavy hair standing over him. Winston checked his watch and sat upright.

"Pardon me, I must have fallen asleep," said Winston groggily.

Stephen smiled. "We didn't want to disturb you. I'm Stephen Lawrence. Perhaps I can give you a tour of the offices tomorrow. We usually leave around four."

"How do you do, Stephen," said Winston standing. He shook Stephen's outstretched hand.

"I suppose I've made some impression on my first day," said Winston apologetically.

"Quite understandable," said Stephen compassionately. "First days can be taxing. Mr. Cohen says that he'll stop by tomorrow morning."

"Arnold was here?" asked Winston.

"Yes, Sir, he didn't want to wake you."

"I want you to know, Mr. Lawrence, that I'm not usually this lax," assured Winston.

"Stephen, Sir, my name is Stephen."

"Stephen it is, and I am Winston. The "Sirs" make me feel like I am a hundred years old."

"Shall I call a cab for you, Winston?" asked Stephen.

"No, thank you, Stephen. Are there any papers that you would like me to take home to look over? I feel like I've wasted an entire afternoon," apologized Winston.

"That won't be necessary. We can start afresh tomorrow. I'll walk you to the elevator."

"I will be eager and ready tomorrow," said Winston with a bit more enthusiasm.

"I'm sure you will," said Stephen.

Chapter XV

The waiting room was filled with women dressed in full, festive skirts and plain blouses. Tidy children with straight, black hair clung to their mothers. It surprised Jonathan to note that the expressions upon the faces of the women and children were contented and amiable. Obviously, they were representatives of Rio's poorest population. Smiles and poverty seemed an absurd incongruity. A young, petite, olive complexioned nurse led Jonathan into the examining room area. "This way, please," said the nurse smiling. Jonathan followed the diminutive young woman through a door that he had never noticed before.

"Where are we going?" asked Jonathan.

"This way, please," repeated the nurse.

They descended a stairway and walked through a brightly-lit tunnel. At the end of the tunnel, Jonathan and the nurse entered a laboratory, where she gave him a dressing gown and pointed to a dressing room. Jonathan held the dressing gown and looked around. Men in white laboratory jackets were consumed with their work examining specimens in Petri dishes. They did not acknowledge his presence.

"This way, please," directed the nurse in a cheerful tone.

"What is all of this?" asked Jonathan curiously.

"Please, you come this way, please," said the nurse taking his arm gently.

They entered a dressing room with green curtains. Jonathan changed into the dressing gown and returned to the lab. A jovial Dr. Halpern approached him.

"Jonathan, it's good to see you. Come with me into my office."

Jonathan followed Dr. Halpern into a rectangular office, which was much smaller than his office on the main floor.

"Please, sit down," said Dr. Halpern motioning towards a plain, wooden chair.

"I don't believe I've ever seen this part of your office," said Jonathan.

"We're expanding," said Dr. Halpern proudly. "Your phone call sounded urgent."

"The tremors are occurring with greater frequency, and they seem to last longer," explained Jonathan.

Dr. Halpern examined Jonathan's chart on his desk. "We can increase the dosage of the pills, but it is only a temporary solution. I'm afraid we may need to progress to stage two sooner than I anticipated."

"I wasn't aware there were stages to this treatment," said Jonathan.

"I'm going to level with you, Jonathan. Your condition is serious and seems to be getting worse. I am going to suggest a radical treatment. I warn you, you may have qualms about the treatment."

"I'm listening," said Jonathan.

"Let's explore the laboratory. I will explain the treatment as we walk," said Dr. Halpern.

He led Jonathan through yet another maze of laboratories, which seemed more sophisticated than the previous one. Many women sat quietly in a waiting area clad in dressing gowns. The women mirrored the other women in the upper office—poor and serene.

"Who are these people?" asked Jonathan.

"Your remedy," said Dr. Halpern. "These women are donors."

Jonathan looked perplexed. "What are they donating?"

"Embryos, Jonathan, they donate their embryos for research purposes, and we pay them."

"They sell their children for medical research? That is unconscionable," said Jonathan with disdain.

"Most of these women have little means to care for additional children, Jonathan. Rather than abort them, they sell the embryos for research," said Dr. Halpern.

"That's absurd. The embryos are still aborted, aren't they?" asked Jonathan watching the smiling women. The thought of their actions repulsed him.

"The idea is repugnant to you, I know," said Dr. Halpern, "but you have never lived in the impoverished conditions these people endure daily. Their donations help people like you regain their health."

"People like me?" asked Jonathan indignantly.

"People of means can afford the newest advancements in medical technology. We are making strides, unbelievable strides. The tissue from the embryos can provide a possible cure for many types of ailments and diseases; this is only the beginning," explained Dr. Halpern as he

led Jonathan through a series of examining rooms, each filled with women ready to undergo procedures that would separate them from their healthy embryos.

"This is stem-cell research, Jonathan. In two or three years, this procedure will be widely-used throughout the world. Millions of people will be saved from the debilitating effects of diabetes, Parkinson's, cancer, and a plethora of other diseases," said Dr. Halpern proudly.

Jonathan stood silently. "How much?" he asked.

"How much what?" answered Dr. Halpern.

"How much do you pay these women for their embryos?" asked Jonathan with a vapid look.

"I see I haven't convinced you," said Dr. Halpern. "Our work here benefits countless people; you will be one of them."

"What happens when the cells are removed from the embryos?" asked Jonathan feeling depleted.

"The procedure is complex, Jonathan. In some instances, the embryos are destroyed. There are other procedures that enable the embryos to live, in which case, the embryos are removed from the uterus, and tissues of some of our clients are added. The embryo is replaced within a healthy uterus and develops normally. The result is a ready source of cells and tissues that can be used to provide the client with the cells needed to ensure continued health and vitality," counseled Dr. Halpern.

Jonathan closed his eyes and breathed deeply.

Dr. Halpern observed his discomfort.

"This research is your hope, Jonathan. Your system is developing an immunity to the herbal treatment. You must consider your options."

"This is not an option," spurned Jonathan. "I will never submit to this unconscionable treatment. I don't know how you live with yourself."

"The question is, will you be able to live with yourself when you are confined to a wheelchair or worse. You are a young man of means, Jonathan. This procedure will enable you to live a normal life. Think about it. You don't need to make a decision today. Stay a few days longer, and let me show you how the procedure works and how it can benefit you."

"I must return home tomorrow," said Jonathan feeling exhausted.

"Will you be able to work or play the cello with an increased frequency of the tremors?" asked Dr. Halpern. "Before you dismiss the procedure, please get all of the information needed to make an informed decision. That is all I ask."

Jonathan reconsidered reluctantly. "All right, I will remain an extra day or two," said Jonathan, "but I assure you that nothing you say will change my opinion of this deplorable manipulation of human life."

Dr. Halpern smiled exuberantly. "Two days will be sufficient; we will begin with a tour of the city."

"I did not come for a tour of the city," said Jonathan impatiently.

"When you visit Rio de Janerio, you are content to remain in the plush hotels, drink the finest wines, and eat the choicest foods. Your only contact with the people of this city is when they are bringing your breakfast on a room service cart or caring for your laundry. Paulita will take you on a tour of areas that you and others like you never get to see. These areas are not included in the packaged tourist tours." The petite nurse stood beside Dr. Halpern. She was so diminutive that Jonathan failed to notice her.

"The expression *you and others like you*" is offensive," said Jonathan.

"These areas will offend your sensibilities even more," said Dr. Halpern sardonically. "I'll see you tomorrow at 9AM. When you return from the tour, you will be ready to visit our state-of-the-art facility. I think that you will find that our research has endless possibilities that will improve the human condition."

Jonathan walked away from Dr. Halpern and his dwarf-like nurse. His hand trembled slightly; he held it steady and tried to obscure the sight of the women in the waiting room from entering his consciousness.

• • •

The ringing phone jarred Stephen's restful sleep. He checked the lighted, emerald-green face of his watch from under the covers and picked up the receiver. The desperate voice on the other end was a disconcertion. "Give me the address," said Stephen as he reached for a pen beside the phone. "Well put someone on who knows the address," said Stephen firmly. "Fine, take her into the police station. I'll be there in about twenty minutes. What is your name? Yes, you may keep the purse, and I'm certain that you will keep the contents as well… I'm sorry, that was rude. Yes, I appreciate your call. Consider the money and the purse your reward…And thank you for notifying me."

Stephen stepped into a pair of wrinkled shorts and a tee shirt. He hastened to the lobby. "I need a cab," he said curtly. The doorman on duty nodded obligingly and stepped outside to hail a taxi. A new doorman held the taxi door open for Stephen and closed it without a smile. Strangely, Stephen missed the smile and the effervescent attitude of the regular doorman, Thornton. Two hours later, the same taxi returned. The unsmiling doorman opened the door for the agitated young man and the drowsy young woman, who was wet and shivering.

"You didn't have to douse me with water," complained Sara as they waited for the elevator.

"You're lucky I didn't call your grandfather," growled Stephen. "How did that woman get my number, anyway?"

"I don't know," answered Sara hesitantly. "It was probably in my purse. You wanted me to call on the hour, remember?"

"Which you failed to do," retorted Stephen.

Stephen helped Sara into the elevator. "Who was that woman? Why did she have your purse, and where are your shoes?" queried Stephen.

"I don't know her name," answered Sara wearily. "She said that you told her to keep my purse as a reward; she wanted my shoes as well."

"You passed out on the subway like a common vagrant," said Stephen with disgust. "Look at yourself." Although her hair was tousled and the majestic blue tank top and matching miniskirt were stained with dirt and wreaked of alcohol, Sara maintained a poise and grace that was emblematic of her finishing school demeanor.

"You might have been killed or worse," said Stephen angrily as the elevator ascended.

Sara snickered. "What can be worse than being killed?"

"In this city, the possibilities are endless," droned Stephen.

"Here's to possibilities," responded Sara holding an imaginary glass and toasting the air.

"Don't be flippant with me, Sara!" admonished Stephen.

"Oh, stop badgering me. You're beginning to sound like Jonathan. We missed my floor. Where are we going? I want to go to my apartment."

"You have no apartment any longer. Henceforth, you'll be monitored by Phillip and me," said Stephen matter-of-factly.

"I'm sleepy, and thanks to you, I'm wet and shivering. I want to take a shower and go to bed," whined Sara.

"You'll shower up here. I'll retrieve your belongings from the apartment. Clearly, you cannot be trusted to remain on your own," said Stephen.

"You'll do no such thing!" shrieked Sara.

Stephen unlocked the door to his apartment and pushed her in.

"You'd better be glad that I'm not taking you to the hospital. There's no telling what has happened to you."

"Nothing happened to me," assured Sara.

"How did you get to Brooklyn, anyway?" asked Stephen. "What's in Brooklyn?"

"I told you, I don't remember," wailed Sara. "Leave me alone and let me go home!"

"You're lying, Sara. With whom did you go to Brooklyn?" persisted Stephen. "You went with those kids from the safari, didn't you? The same ones you spent every day drinking and with, didn't you?"

"I didn't go with anyone. I went alone to get away from you, the cameras, and this prison," yelled Sara.

"The doorman didn't call me when you left. He helped you, didn't he? How much did you pay him?" demanded Stephen.

"Leave me alone!" yelled Sara. "I'm cold and tired, and I'm wet, thanks to you! If you don't let me out of here, I'll call my grandfather and tell him how you're treating me."

"That is a splendid idea," remarked Stephen. "While you're at it, tell him how you have been sneaking out of the apartment, drinking, and sleeping on subways in unspeakable areas. Tell him how you ended up in a police station without your purse or shoes. I'll call your grandfather myself, and he will place you in a hospital, where you will finally get the help you need!"

"You think that I need to be in a hospital?" fumed Sara. "What about Jonathan? Why do you think he hasn't returned? It's been over a week, hasn't it? He hasn't told you, has he? If you call my grandfather, I'll tell him about Jonathan, and it will be your fault, Stephen. It will be your fault, and Jonathan will hate you!"

Stephen placed his cell phone on an end table. "Call whomever you wish."

Sara grabbed the phone and threw it at Stephen.

"I hate you!" she yelled.

"Take a shower and wash your hair; it's matted, or haven't you noticed? You'd better be glad that I was at home. You're underage, and you can get your family into a lot of trouble. They deserve better from you, Sara," asserted Stephen.

"I hate all of you!" screamed Sara running into the bathroom.

Phillip exited his bedroom rubbing his eyes groggily. "What's going on?"

"Don't let Sara leave this apartment. I'll be right back," said Stephen.

"What's she doing here?" asked Phillip.

"Just make sure that she doesn't leave." Stephen took his keys and closed the door. The words *Jonathan* and *hospital* would not leave Stephen's thoughts. He hoped against hope that it was the remnants of the alcohol speaking, but deep within, he knew that Sara was telling the truth.

Upon entering Jonathan's apartment, Stephen hastened to Jonathan's room. It was meticulous. Nothing was out of place. If any clues were to be found, they would not be found in Jonathan's immaculate room. The light blinked cheerfully on the answering machine. Stephen retrieved the message. Daniel Cohen and his wife, Elizabeth, had returned from a restful visit to Greece and would be visiting their son and their daughter on Thursday.

Stephen remembered his first meeting with Daniel Cohen. The heir apparent to Cohen Enterprises was suave, urbane, and confident, or so Stephen thought. How quickly things unraveled. Within the course of a year, Stephen watched the man who had hired him devolve into a pathetic creature without a position in his own corporation. It was ironic. Stephen, the intern, was now in charge of his own division, and Daniel Cohen had been demoted. Corporate finance was a treacherous world, but it was the only world for Stephen Lawrence. He knew how to play the game as craftily as the moguls with whom he came into contact, but he adopted none of their ways. Money was nothing unless it was rooted in service. Daniel Cohen did not understand that, but his father, Arnold Cohen, did. Daniel desired fame and fortune; Arnold envisioned a global community rooted in sacrificial service. Arnold saw through the professional exterior into Stephen's interior heart of a servant. The environmental and social programs were thriving under his care. What would happen to the programs when he returned to the university? Surely, Winston Brielle would not be able to handle things. He could barely stay awake through the afternoon. The other assistants would be returning to their prospective colleges and universities as well. Stephen knew that he was trying to distract himself. He did not want to think of the words *Jonathan* and *hospital*, and he wanted to purge his mind of the image of Sara standing helplessly before him in the wet tank top and miniskirt at the police station. He thought back to the first time he saw her at her graduation party dressed in frills and lace. What happened to change the innocent ingénue? The words *Jonathan* and *hospital* became intertwined with the words *Sara* and *hospital*. Both siblings were ill and in need of professional help. Why did the well being of both Jonathan and Sara rest upon his inexperienced shoulders?

Stephen opened the door to Sara's bedroom and could not suppress a gasp of horror. The room smelled rancid. Bugs crawled over dirty dishes, and piles of dirty clothes were strewn across the unmade bed. Half-eaten cartons of take-out food dripped various liquids and discolored food onto the stained carpet. Drained bottles of an assortment of alcoholic beverages decorated the carpet like colorful game board tokens. Stephen shook his head in utter disbelief. He ventured into the filth and opened the chest of drawers and the closet; both were empty. Stephen angrily returned to his apartment to confront Sara, but she slept soundly on the sofa wrapped in a towel while Phillip watched television.

"Sara, get up!" said Stephen shaking her.

"She's out," said Phillip. "Nothing can wake her." Freemont nestled next to Sara on the towel. The sight of the trusting canine and the reckless ingénue touched a compassionate chord within Stephen. He covered Sara with a blanket and returned to her apartment. Stephen sorted Sara's dirty clothes into color-coded piles near the compact washer-dryer in the kitchen and began the monumental task of cleaning Sara's room and washing her clothes.

Streams of sunlight rested on the large garbage bags near the front door. Sara's freshly-laundered clothes were placed neatly in the closet and the chest of drawers. The room was clean and fragrant. Even the bedspread and sheets had been laundered. If Sara inquired as to the whereabouts of any of her belongings, Stephen would refer her to the trash bin. There was little time for sorting and saving; the entire apartment was now presentable for Daniel and Elizabeth Cohen's visit. Stephen left the door to Sara's room open for a final airing and checked his watch. The apartment was ready, but Stephen could not trust Sara to remain alcohol free until her parent's visit. She was in no condition to return to the office. Stephen was usually on the train to the office at six o'clock, but today, he would remain with Sara until her parents arrived. With the elder Cohen in San Francisco, Stephen was not ready to trust the unstable Daniel Cohen and his mercenary wife with the plights of their children.

Returning to his apartment, Stephen found Phillip dressed and ready to leave for work. Sara remained on the sofa sleeping soundly. Freemont nestled on the blanket and watched her sleep.

"Where have you been?" asked Phillip. "I haven't taken Freemont out for fear that she might awaken and leave. What are we going to do with her?"

"I'll stay with her," said Stephen.

"That doesn't make any sense," said Stephen. "How can you help her? Sara needs professional help, Stephen. We must call someone to come and get her. She won't have to spend another night here, will she?"

"I'll handle it," said Stephen with irritation.

"You're trying to handle too much, if you ask me," intoned Phillip.

Stephen attached Freemont's leash to his collar and handed him to Phillip. "You can take him out now. He'll be more of a help in the office than she ever was."

"Come on, Freemont," said Phillip. He placed Freemont under his arm, and they left for work.

Stephen sat on the edge of the sofa and watched Sara sleep. He brushed the hair from Sara's face with his hand. Stephen moved closer and observed her face and the aristocratic features that defined the sleeping beauty. Jonathan shared those aristocratic features, as did all of the Cohen men, though they were more delicate and refined in the beautiful face Stephen observed. He touched Sara's long, sandy hair, which felt tangled and matted in places. How long had she allowed herself to devolve into a state of disrepair? Strangely, he did not see Sara when he looked at Jonathan, but he saw Jonathan when he looked at Sara. She possessed his eyes, his nose, and the quirky smile that emerged whenever he attempted sarcasm. Stephen combed and brushed Sara's hair gently as she slept hoping not to wake her. There was a helplessness about her that proved to be irresistible. Her sleeping expression was tranquil and peaceful. A calming presence emanated from both Jonathan and Sara; no matter what the circumstance, their worlds remained unfettered. The forces of nature seemed to work in tandem to promote a sense of serenity, well being, and a suitable outcome for any dilemma. Stephen touched her bare shoulders, and feelings stirred within him that he had not experienced for quite some time. Stephen lay beside her on the sofa and touched her face,

Jonathan's face. Somehow the two were inextricably linked. He held her close and slept a peaceful sleep beside his imaginary salmacistic concoction.

•   •   •

Sara stirred at noonday thirsting for a drink and craving for a cigarette. She found herself wrapped in the embrace of the sleeping Stephen. She smiled. "I knew it!" thought Sara removing the towel that separated them. "You didn't believe me, dear brother, but I told you so." Sara wrapped herself around Stephen as he slept. The desire for a drink and a cigarette waned in the midst of this new development. Sara kissed Stephen until he awoke. He was startled to find himself locked within her embrace.

"What are you doing?" asked Stephen with trepidation as she removed his tee shirt and kissed his chest. "Stop that, you demon!"

Sara kissed Stephen's words away, and he allowed her to continue until her passion became his passion as well.

Afternoon sunbeams glowed over the twosome. For Sara, it was a sign, a blessing of sorts, and the illumination of a bright, new future. For Stephen, the revelatory sunbeams ensconced him within a life that he thought was an irretrievable past. A guilt-laden cloud overshadowed him, and he uttered a mournful sigh.

"If you must blame someone, blame me," said Sara sitting up and allowing the sunbeams to immerse her body.

"I'm not blaming anyone," said Stephen remorsefully.

"I'm going to my apartment. I need a cigarette and a drink." She kissed Stephen victoriously.

"You won't find anything there," said Stephen recalling the deplorable condition of her apartment. "I threw everything away."

A sense of urgency rushed through Sara. "What do you mean?"

"I cleaned your room and threw everything into the trash," said Stephen. "There will be no more drinking or smoking. Phillip and I will continue to monitor you to ensure that you don't regress."

Sara closed her eyes and clenched the towel that lay beside her feet. "I thought that everything would change," she said softly.

"Everything *has* changed," confirmed Stephen, "but I won't let you destroy yourself or compromise Jonathan."

"You think that *I* have compromised Jonathan?" shrieked Sara. "The utter gall and arrogance."

"All right, we are both responsible," admitted Stephen, "but we don't have to make it worse."

"What are you saying, Stephen?" asked Sara exhaustedly.

Stephen ran his fingers through his hair anxiously. "I don't know," said Stephen. "When I see you, I see Jonathan. When I touch you, I touch Jonathan. It is as though you share the same essence—the same inner being. You're both connected in such a way that I don't feel that I have lost him."

"Well, you can't have both of us, Stephen," said Sara with irritation.

"I know," said Stephen tortuously. "Look, I don't know what will happen in the future. We have today, and that is all we can expect."

"I need a drink," said Sara with exasperation.

"That is the first time you admitted that you need the alcohol," said Stephen.

"What do you want me to do?" cried Sara.

"I want you to need me," said Stephen gently pulling her beside him, "even if it's just for today. We can help each other until we figure everything out."

In the gleam of the cheerful, afternoon sunbeams and the light of the hidden cameras, they nourished and sustained one another.

• • •

The patter of the rain upon the luxuriant leaves inhabiting the rain forest grew more intense. The intermittent squeal of a bird breached the symphonic tones of rain cascading down the leaves of flourishing tropical greenery. Diffident thunder growled ambiguously. Jonathan Cohen sat on the saturated ground under an umbrella of leaves and vines. The rain streamed down his face and smooth, black hair. His clothes, saturated with mild, fragrant water pressed against his flesh. Jonathan's vacuous stare gave the impression of a man who had recently returned from the dead. Stephen's words were as revelatory as they were nonsensical.

The thought that one could see Jonathan in Sara and Sara in Jonathan was not really unusual. They were, after all, brother and sister, but the idea that the two could embody the same essence, spirit, or inner being was an absurdity. *When I touch you, I touch Jonathan.* Had Stephen gone mad? Jonathan cursed the cameras, and then he cursed himself and his illness. The tour of the disenfranchised areas of Rio de Janerio left him with a sense of devastation, but in light of recent events, Jonathan's righteous indignation turned into practical mediation. Surely, he could make a donation to some charity to help to ease the plight of the people. He needed his health in order to halt Stephen's growing attachment to Sara. Jonathan's hand began to quiver slightly as he reached for his cell phone. His tremulous hand held the phone to his ear. Dr. Halpern was elated to receive the call and mobilized his eager researchers to begin the search for a donor.

Chapter XVI

Daniel and Elizabeth Cohen arrived promptly at eight. Sara, rested and cheerful, let her parents into the apartment and brought them glasses of lemonade. Neither the apartment nor Sara showed signs of the chaos of the previous evening. Stephen joined the Cohens on the sofa. Freemont climbed onto Daniel's lap and waited to be stroked.

"I hear you've done tremendous things on the eighty-second floor with the new programs, Stephen," said Daniel.

"Thank you, Sir, but I didn't do it alone," said Stephen modestly.

Daniel chuckled. "I know my son well enough to know that you, indeed, managed to get those programs off the ground alone. How many employees are working up there now?"

"Around twenty-six, if you include the new employee, Mr. Brielle," said Stephen.

"Did you say Brielle?" asked Daniel.

"Yes, Winston Brielle started working as a consultant last week," said Stephen.

"How interesting. Did you hear that, Elizabeth? Winston Brielle is working for his son's strongest adversary. You'd better watch him, Stephen. I know that Brielle and my father are close friends, but he is still Sheridon Southgate's father."

"Mr. Brielle fell asleep on his first day, didn't he, Stephen?" laughed Sara.

Stephen eyed her cautiously and spoke with a controlled voice. "Mr. Brielle is a competent administrator. He is in charge of our new Computers-in-Schools Program."

"Really?" asked Elizabeth. "I don't think I've heard of that program."

"It was Jonathan's idea," said Stephen. "The program will bring busloads of inner city students into the office to let them see how computers function in the workplace."

"Yes," said Sara excitedly, "and we're going to have a grand celebration in September to get the program started. You two should come."

"Your father can go" said Elizabeth warily. "I have no desire to watch a busload of screaming inner-city children dismantle the corporation. You'd better watch the computers and the other office equipment, Stephen. You know how those kids are."

"That's enough, Elizabeth," admonished Daniel.

"It's true, and you know it. They'll steal everything that is not nailed down," warned Elizabeth.

Daniel shook his head in disgust. "Can't you keep a civil tongue at least through the evening?"

"Come on, Mom and Dad, let's have some of Stephen's special herb rice," mediated Sara.

"Herb rice? What is that, some kind of Indian dish? I don't like Indian food. There's a nice French restaurant on Madison. Why don't we go there?" asked Elizabeth.

"Stephen has already cooked," protested Sara.

"We can eat out, if you like," said Stephen pleasantly.

"We'll eat here," insisted Daniel, "and I would love to attend the festivities for the children in September. In fact, if there is anything I can do to help, just let me know."

"Great," said Stephen. I'll tell Winston. I'm sure he will be delighted." Stephen led the Cohens to the dining area. "Where's Sara?"

"I don't know," said Elizabeth taking a seat opposite her husband, who made himself comfortable at the head of the table. "She disappeared into her room."

Stephen winced. "Please excuse me." He hurried to Sara's room and knocked on the locked door gently. "Sara, we need you out here," called Stephen through the door."

"I'll be right out," answered Sara from within.

"Open the door, Sara, right now," whispered Stephen. There was no reply. "Sara, let me in. What are you doing in there?" asked Stephen authoritatively.

Elizabeth smiled at her husband and whispered. "You see, I told you that there was nothing wrong with him. I thought that he and Jonathan…well, I think I sense sparks between the Sara and Stephen."

"There is nothing wrong with my son!" said Daniel firmly. "You think that everyone is either gay or a thief."

"Look at the way he's holding Sara's arm and escorting her to the table like a gentleman," whispered Elizabeth smiling. "I think that you are going to get your wish. You wanted them to get together, remember?"

Stephen led Sara to the ladderback chair and pulled it out for her. His fingerprints were still on her arm from the tightness of his grip. "I'm sure you'll be comfortable here next to your mother. I'll just relieve you of this," said Stephen taking her bedroom key from her hand. "You wouldn't want your parents to see the condition of your room, would you?" Stephen sat on the other side of Sara.

Elizabeth smiled. "You're wasting your time, Stephen, if you think that Sara will ever keep a tidy room. Don't worry, we know that our little princess is a bit of a slob. I must say, you're a chivalrous young man, Stephen, and you've taken such good care of Sara in everyone's absence. What kind of wine are we having with dinner? We had the most delectable Greek wine in Athens, didn't we, Darling? What was the name of it?"

"No wine," said Stephen curtly. "I'm sorry, but I prepared lemonade and iced tea." He corrected his tone. "Sara, why don't you get the beverages while I bring the rice?"

"I don't want any rice. I want wine. We always have wine with dinner," said Sara with agitation, Isn't that right, Mother?"

"Well, if Stephen would rather not," said Elizabeth, "I suppose we can do without the wine for one night. Sara *does* love her dinner wine. She started drinking it at...how old were you, Dear?"

"Five, Mom. I was five-years-old when we pretended that we were in France, where the children drink wine with every meal," said Sara.

"Of course," said Elizabeth reminiscing, "what fun we had."

"We don't have any wine," insisted Stephen.

"Well, why don't I just go out and get a bottle of burgundy. Burgundy goes with rice, doesn't it?" asked Daniel.

Stephen placed the steaming herb rice on the table. "Dinner is served. We have salad and bread also."

"Oh, well then, I suppose we should dig in," said Daniel placing a spoonful of herb rice onto his plate. "Too bad Jonathan is missing all of this. When did you say he'll be returning?"

"Tomorrow evening, Sir," said Stephen passing the rice to Mrs. Cohen. The mention of Jonathan's return filled Stephen with anxiety.

"He's missing quite a treat. He won't find anything like this in Nevada," said Daniel tasting the rice cheerfully.

"Heat and insects are all he'll find out there," said Elizabeth. "I can't imagine why he would want his group to perform out in the wilderness. Prairie dogs, gamblers, and Indians—that's all he'll find out there. The people out there couldn't possibly enjoy chamber music. I've never heard of anything so outrageous, have you, Dear?" asked Elizabeth looking at Sara.

"Oh, I can think of a few things," said Sara placing her hand on Stephen's thigh under the table. "The world is full of outrageous things. Jonathan will return tomorrow, and find that there is no dinner wine chilling in the refrigerator. He will find the very notion outrageous, won't he, Mother?"

Elizabeth smiled. "Now, Dear, everyone doesn't share our customs. Perhaps the idea of wine with dinner is new to Stephen."

"That's enough, Elizabeth," said Daniel angrily. He took his napkin from his lap and placed it on the table. "I'm not hungry anymore."

"You let the smallest things upset you," said Elizabeth. "I'm merely suggesting that Stephen will grow to appreciate our customs when he gets to know us a little better. I'm certain that between Jonathan and Sara, he will be initiated fully into our little family."

Stephen's iced tea caught in his throat. Sara used his napkin to wipe the liquid from his face. "Yes," she said smiling, "between Jonathan and I, Stephen will be initiated fully into this little family."

Chapter XVII

The telephones rang incessantly in the Southgate hotel suite. Office personnel flounced in and out of adjoining rooms inhabited with serious looking men clad in dark suits gazing at computer screens. Sheridon exited one of the rooms with a pair of glasses poised atop his sandy hair wearing a pea green tee shirt with a small alligator emblazoned on the left, a pair of navy blue shorts, and leather thong sandals. Obviously, it was not the mogul's intention to remain in the corporate suite for any appreciable length of time.

"Mike, get in here!" bellowed Sheridon.

A gentleman with speckled gray hair entered the room. Sheridon thrust a handful of papers into his accountant's hands. "You're the accountant. Account for this. These figures fall well below our bottom line." The gentleman stood dumbfounded. "I want these figures back in ten minutes," said Sheridon impatiently, "and I want them to total our anticipated bottom line." Mike took the papers and reentered the adjoining door with a look of exasperation. The usually cheerful Sheridon was not having a good day. On troublesome days, he was wont to fire people without provocation. Everyone moved carefully in his presence.

"Mr. Lawrence and Ms. Cohen are here," announced his administrative assistant gingerly.

"Send them into Suite A, and get me cup of latte," ordered Sheridon.

The youthful assistant gripped her pencil and prepared for the tumult. "The latte machine is broken, Sheridon" lamented the unfortunate woman. Sheridon looked askance up at the ceiling.

"I've ordered a new one," she added quickly, "but it won't arrive before tomorrow morning. I'm sorry." Sheridon cast an icy gaze at his assistant. "There's a Starbucks in the building next door. I can go and bring a cup of latte," offered the assistant eagerly.

"Do I look like I want a cup? Tell them to send the machine," barked Sheridon as he entered Suite A. The assistant looked at Sheridon incredulously.

"Yes, Sir," said the assistant timorously.

Sheridon tinkered with the laptop on his desk as Stephen and Sara entered his office. "Please, sit down," said Sheridon without looking at them. Sara and Stephen sat close together on the comfortable sofa. Sheridon frowned at his laptop. "No matter how infallible people claim these contraptions are, they can do nothing without input from fallible human hands. Can I get you anything—sodas," Sheridon turned his gaze towards Sara, "or something stronger?"

"Nothing, thank you," responded Stephen.

"Oh, forgive me. Of course, Ms. Cohen is not old enough to indulge in alcoholic beverages. Perhaps you'd like something, Stephen."

"I prefer to be called Mr. Lawrence," said Stephen indignantly.

"Then Mr. Lawrence it shall be." Jonathan poured himself a glass of wine and sipped it as he watched his guests. "I suppose you're wondering why I invited both of you here, as well you might. I have a problem that you may be able to assist me in solving."

Stephen looked quizzically. "There are many experienced people working for you in this suite—why call us?"

"I don't know anything about business," added Sara, "and I wouldn't help you anyway. My grandfather hates you."

"Ah, yes, the venerable Arnold Cohen," said Sheridon." I see that you have inherited his lack of tact."

"What do you want, Southgate?" asked Stephen caustically.

"I prefer to be called Mr. Southgate," said Sheridon. "I think that we can assist one another amicably. I am going to merge Bentley Wireless with my wireless conglomerates. The merger will make me the strongest competitor in wireless services in the United States and Europe."

"That's not news, Mr. Southgate. Everyone knows about the proposed merger. How does that concern us?" asked Stephen.

"Sources indicate that Bentley Wireless, a staunchly conservative establishment in London with an unreasonable penchant for family values, will be made privy to photographs, which capture me in, shall we say, a rather compromising position, before the final papers are signed next week."

"Why tell us?" asked Stephen.

"Arnold Cohen will use those photographs to discredit me. Of course, I will use everything within my power to avert any unpleasant actions," ensured Sheridon.

"Once again, why tell us?" asked Stephen.

"You are the intellect behind the summer initiatives program at Cohen Enterprises—my compliments. You have incorporated social service programs, environmental programs, and now a school computer program. You are quite an asset to the Cohen team, Mr. Lawrence. It is a shame that all of your efforts will be wasted when you leave in September. You are still planning to complete your final year of graduate school, aren't you?"

"Of course," replied Stephen "but why does that concern you?"

"My corporation is involved with medical research. I once considered a medical career, albeit in dentistry. Did you know that?" asked Sheridon.

"I'm sorry, Mr. Southgate, but I really don't know why this is of any concern to us," said Stephen. "I don't know why you're wasting our time with any of it. We can't help you."

"I would like you and the young lady to use your influence with Arnold Cohen to prevent those photographs from circulating. You are a valued intern and have established initiatives that have the potential to propel Cohen Enterprises as a formidable civic and environmental force within the city," said Sheridon.

"I'm afraid you overestimate my position in the corporation. I have no influence over Mr. Cohen," said Stephen.

"And you underestimate your influence with his grandchildren," said Sheridon.

Sara laughed. "You must be out of your mind if you think that my brother and I will help you."

"Jonathan Cohen is gravely ill," said Sheridon. He dropped a manila envelope on the desk with a thud. "These are his medical records. Would you like to see them?"

"Where did you get those?" asked Stephen anxiously.

"I can help him. My researchers are on the brink of discoveries that can change modern medicine as we know it. There are procedures that can help to control the effects of devastating diseases," said Sheridon proudly, "and we can use them to help Jonathan and others in need of a miracle."

Stephen and Sara looked at the manila envelope on the desk.

"What kind of diseases?" asked Stephen.

"Let us say that Jonathan's holistic treatments, which take him to Brazil each month, can benefit from the research and procedures performed in my laboratories," said Sheridon smugly.

"If the research is legitimate, why isn't it performed here in the United States?" asked Stephen.

"You are quite astute, Mr. Lawrence," said Sheridon. " It takes years to gain approval for some of the advances that we have already made. I don't think that Jonathan can wait. I am also concerned that young Mr. Cohen might not be enamoured with your relationship with his sister. Farbeit from me to judge you, but any undue stress and strain is likely to hinder the effectiveness of the procedure."

"I think that we've heard enough," said Stephen angrily." I don't know what you're doing, but my relationship with Sara is none of your concern. If your words are veiled threats to inform Jonathan, you can save them. We will tell him ourselves when he returns. And another thing, I hope that the authorities put an end to those sleazy mystical potions of yours. They're preventing Jonathan from seeking help from competent physicians. Come on, Sara." Stephen and Sara walked toward the door.

"When was the last time you heard Jonathan play that cello of his?" asked Sheridon. "I think he calls it Mitzi. Those sleazy, mystical potions, as you refer to them, are helping Jonathan to lead a normal life. It is easy for you to walk away, Mr. Lawrence, you seem to be enjoying the best of both worlds."

"I hate you!" yelled Sara.

Sheridon smiled. "I am accustomed to the hate. It's the love that seems to present the most serious problems."

"What do you want?" asked Stephen as his shoulders slumped in surrender.

"You know what I want, Mr. Lawrence. I would like the merger to go forth without incident next week in exchange for your friend, Jonathan's, quality of life. I can guarantee that the treatments he is receiving in Brazil will help him to live a normal life."

"Yes, but normal at what human cost?" asked Stephen.

"What difference does it make?" asked Sheridon." You are able to live normally. Do you think that Jonathan and others like him care about the human costs? They want to function normally. I'm willing to jeopardize all that I have to help them."

"Come on, Southgate. Since when do you care about anything that doesn't have a dollar sign attached?" asked Stephen.

"It is quite true that my motives are not entirely altruistic, nor should they be. I am a financier first and foremost. If I can make a sizable profit and help my fellowman along the way, why not?" asked Sheridon reasonably.

"I can't guarantee anything," said Stephen.

"I am not asking for guarantees. Your effort will suffice. I am certain that you will be successful, Mr. Lawrence. I admonish you not to mention this to anyone. If the FDA is informed, my laboratories will be closed, and the research will end. There will be serious legal ramifications for me, but the consequences for Jonathan will be dire. I must insist upon your silence."

Stephen opened the door for Sara to exit first. They walked quietly to the elevator, out of which a large café latte machine was being transported to the Southgate Suite.

Sara turned around to find Sheridon standing in the doorway with a knowing smile upon his face.

"Don't look back," said Stephen.

"What are we going to do?" asked Sara. She longed for a cigarette and a drink. Without thinking, she turned again. Sheridon smiled and entered his suite behind the latte machine. He closed the door softly. Stephen sighed as they stepped onto the elevator.

• • •

Stephen and Sara entered the darkened apartment and proceeded to the bedroom in silence. Freemont, normally greeting them, had retired for a mischievous respite, no doubt, in Jonathan's room between the pillow shams adorning the bed, which were off-limits when Jonathan was at home. No attempt was made to check phone messages, pull the drapes, or turn on the lights. Stephen remembered to disable the cameras, for it was time to strengthen the bond they shared before the impending turmoil. Jonathan's rancor would erupt through unpredictable channels. The Cohen family would greet the news of Stephen's dual relationships with vehement repugnance. The ensuing protestations would be intolerable for the fragile Sara. Stephen noted her backward glance towards Sheridon Southgate after their meeting and was certain that her vacillating fortitude had not escaped the mogul's keen observation. Stephen would strengthen her emotionally and physically, but the incertitude of Sara's conviction to retain an unwavering stance in favor of the troublous relationship filled him with a sense of disconcertion. They lay quietly upon her bed in the dark, sensing one another's trepidation. As Stephen held her close to his heart, he tried to identify the pivotal point, at which the relationship mushroomed from one of obligatory care-taking to one of irrepressible passion and commitment. There was something about Sara that evoked images of Jonathan, and thoughts of intimate moments with Jonathan were now ensconced with visions of Sara. For the first time, Stephen realized that he desired and loved both siblings. In twenty-four hours, Jonathan would return, and Stephen would be forced to choose. There was but one recourse; he would venture forth alone. As Stephen and Sara shared the most passionate love of their relationship, they neither saw nor heard Jonathan emerge from his bedroom and walk silently out of the front door carrying the suitcase, with which he had arrived two hours prior.

Chapter XVIII

Morning broke through the uncovered windows like a warrior with a ray of sun as its lance. The sunlight pierced Stephen's forehead, and he was awakened from a discontented sleep to find that Sara was not lying beside him. There was a note on the night stand. Sara knew that he would not be able to make a choice, so she would make it for him. She would bow out and leave him to love and care for her ailing brother. Stephen returned the note to the night stand. For the first time, he realized that Sara was not the spoiled, irrational creature he grew to love; she was a person who could love and sacrifice for the love she felt and shared readily. Stephen hastened to the substitute doorman, but he could not or would not yield any clues as to Sara's departure. Jonathan would be arriving, and Stephen did not want to be in the apartment when he arrived. He entered the apartment that he shared with Phillip. There were no messages.

"You may as well go to the office," said Phillip. "Jonathan will probably go there if you aren't here."

"How did I get entangled in all of this?" asked Stephen.

"Don't ask me," said Phillip. "I haven't been able to figure you out since you met those two. You're not yourself. You need a break. Why don't you take some time off and then sort everything out?"

"I can't," said Stephen. "Sara is out there somewhere. I don't know what she'll do."

"You said that the note was rational. She'll grow up and move on," said Phillip.

"What if she doesn't? What if it's all an act?" asked Stephen.

"Well, what if it is? There isn't anything you can do about it now," said Phillip. "Go to the office and take your mind off of everything. You'll be able to think clearly when you return and face Jonathan. What are you going to tell him anyway? Is it over between you and Sara, or what?"

Stephen sighed. "I want her, but she's right. It would kill Jonathan. I'm walking away from both."

"Old man Cohen will be furious when he finds out," said Phillip. "Someone's bound to tell him."

"I'll tell him myself," said Stephen.

"No, don't do that," warned Phillip, "at least not until the end of the summer. He'll shut down the programs, and we'll all be out of work. We'll have to leave these apartments, and most of us don't have anywhere to go. Come on, Stephen, don't say anything yet. This may all blow over."

"When did everything get so complicated?" asked Stephen.

"I don't know," said Phillip, "but the ball is in your court. Don't drop it."

"I'd better get Freemont out of the apartment and bring him up here. We can take him to work with us," said Stephen.

Jonathan and Sara's apartment door was open. Stephen left in such haste, he forgot to close it. Stephen feared that Freemont might have wandered out, but he breathed a sigh of relief when he saw the trusty canine playing with a ball in the living room.

"Come on, boy, let's go out for a walk." Stephen placed the leash on Freemont's collar, and they started for the door. Something caught his attention and he turned towards Jonathan's room. The door was open. "Have you been playing in there, you bad boy? You know Jonathan likes everything to be in place. He'll be here today, you know. I'd better check to see what mischief you've gotten into in there." Stephen dropped the leash and walked into Jonathan's room. The drapes were drawn. Stephen wondered if Sara had closed them before she left. Why would she do that? Stephen's eyes wandered around the room. The bedspread was slightly rumpled as though someone had been lying on it. Jonathan's slippers and robe were out of the closet. They both lay on the floor. That was most unusual. Stephen's heart began to pound. He noticed the papers on Jonathan's dresser. There were airline and hotel receipts. Stephen checked the date and the time on the return airline ticket. His heart beat against his chest as he realized that Jonathan must have been in the apartment when he and Sara returned from Sheridon Southgate's office. Had Jonathan spoken with Sara before she left? Did he force her decision? Where were they? Were they together plotting against him, or were they alone, each facing their own private misery? Stephen breathed deeply. His imagination was getting the better of him. He took three deep breaths, picked up the leash, and walked Freemont to the elevator. His world was crumbling around him; he held the fate of too many people in his youthful hands. Stephen wished that he could turn back the clock to leisurely walks across campus with serious students eager to enter the business world. If he could go back in time, he would warn them of the pitfalls. He would tell them to hold onto their youthful, carefree days. The world of business was a complicated world, and he was about to find out how complications can destroy dreams. Dear Reader, it is at times like these that the only true comfort is in the warmth and unconditional love of a canine friend. Stephen held Freemont close as they entered the elevator. Freemont licked Stephen's cheek and nestled his head against Stephen's chest.

• • •

The walls of the office were adorned with framed artwork that Nigel took the liberty of selecting, as Stephen Lawrence did not appear to be a patron of the arts. Nigel adjusted one of the sketches as Stephen entered, glasses over his curly, brown hair, and sat behind his desk engrossed in an environmental report. Nigel did not wait for an applausive response to his endeavors; he understood that Stephen would be content with bare walls. Jonathan, on the other hand, took pains to collaborate and offer suggestions regarding the artwork and sculpture that graced his environ. Stephen was not of Jonathan's ilk, to be sure, but Nigel was aghast that the cretin did not take the time to look upon the beauteous works of art illuminating the drab office. Stephen felt Nigel's eyes watching him and looked up from the report. "Is something wrong, Nigel?" asked Stephen.

"I wondered whether the paintings and sketches were to your liking. Without a clear indication of your interests, I was compelled to use my own discretion," said Nigel.

Stephen glanced around the office rapidly. "Sure, sure, they're fine, Nigel—very pretty. Has Jonathan been in the office today?"

"No," said Nigel adjusting one of the paintings, "I haven't seen him. Do you want me to try to reach him?"

"No, "responded Stephen emphatically. Nigel turned and looked at him questionably.

"No, thank you," said Stephen adjusting his tone. "I'll try to reach him later. Who is scheduled to make the presentation to the New York Environmental Society this afternoon?"

"I believe Phillip has been assigned," said Nigel.

"Ask him to come in, will you? Thanks, Nigel, and thanks for the pictures," said Stephen without looking at them.

"Of course," said Nigel with a tone of condescension.

As the assistant exited the room, Stephen's gaze shifted from the report to a drawing that entered his peripheral vision. His eyes focused upon the curious representation as he walked slowly towards its captivating aura. "Nigel?" called Stephen. Nigel appeared in the doorway with Phillip. Stephen's eyes did not leave the drawing.

"Yes?" answered Nigel calmly.

"What is that?" asked Stephen. Nigel and Phillip entered the office and stood before the drawing.

Phillip was agog. He clasped his hands and remarked, "Ah! Where ever did you find it? It is exquisite!" Phillip touched the gilded frame as he admired the drawing.

"It wasn't easy," rendered Nigel, "but I persevered. The Fogg Museum of Art was quite helpful. Jonathan ordered it a few weeks ago; It arrived yesterday."

A few of the office workers appeared in the doorway. They approached the drawing as though it was something sacred.

Stephen took his glasses from his hair and placed them over his nose. "What is this thing, Nigel?" asked Stephen. He stood before the drawing with furled eyebrows.

Pleased that Stephen had, at last, noticed the glorious representation, Nigel endeavored to provide a descriptive analysis of the work. "In this drawing," said Nigel gleefully, "Jupiter has transformed himself into an eagle and is ascending with the splendorous Ganymede in tow. The youth will become his cupbearer."

"It's obscene!" declared Stephen with disgust.

"It's Michelangelo," corrected Phillip as he and the other office workers gathered around Michelangelo's masterpiece to admire its majesty.

Stephen's eyes squinted as he attempted to see the beauty that mesmerized the others. The naked Ganymede, clutched by the forceful wings and talons of the eagle, did not appear to resist its penetrating domination. Stephen found Michelangelo's classic the most horrifying, homoerotic artwork that he had ever beheld, and he could not imagine sharing an office with it.

"Is it not to your liking?" inquired Nigel after noting Stephen's perplexed expression. "Fear not, I'll place it in Jonathan's office." Nigel removed the drawing from the wall.

"I'm sorry, Nigel," said Stephen, "I guess I'm not the eagle wings/ naked guy type. How about getting me a picture of a horse or the sky or something like this one?" Stephen hastened to the framed Monet. "This one is nice and simple. Your taste is impeccable. Why don't we place these watery flowers over here?" Stephen removed the Monet from the wall and placed it in the space vacated by Michelangelo's image of the soul merging with the divine. "There, now I'm a connoisseur of art," teased Stephen.

Nigel smiled with feigned amusement and exited the office with Michelangelo's *jewel* in hand. Phillip and the other office workers followed him to Jonathan's empty office and admired its new home. Alas, Dear Reader, Stephen did not realize that art and life were inextricably linked; as a consequence, he was unable to circumvent the calamitous events that would irrevocably transform his life.

• • •

The sun hid playfully behind the clouds and pretended to enjoy a brief respite from the toil of illuminating the skyscrapers. The mammoth creatures lacked humility; the sun would show them who the avatar of light in town was. The artificial vestiges of twinkling lights cast an appalling temporal festivity throughout the city, but without the sun, the city lights were Christmas ornaments in August—ostensibly out of season. Summer required the dazzling sun to provide the effervescence that was the city. The mischievous sun protruded from the dense clouds and flexed its muscles once more before settling down to a peaceful night's sleep, for the moon was in top form also and would show those lights a thing or two.

Sunbeams nudged the woman's hand at the top of the stairs to the subway station as she searched for a Metro Card. Tissues, lipstick, and keys fell to the pavement as the woman rummaged through the recalcitrant purse. She cursed softly and proceeded unsteadily down the stairs.

"Ten dollar Metro Card," announced the dazed woman as she slid a bill through the small opening of the window.

"Miss, you forgot your change," yelled the clerk through the glass as the woman used the Metro Card to gain entrance through the stall. The clerk summoned a transit policeman. Clearly, the purse did not belong to the woman, and she was too intoxicated to realize that she had given the clerk a hundred dollar bill. The transit policeman questioned the woman, whose responses were predictably unintelligible.

"Are you Sara Cohen?" asked the officer audibly over the roar of the departing train. The woman laughed and murmured a response, which the officer could not decipher. Another officer approached.

"What do we have here?" asked the officer surveying the woman's rumpled attire and unstable demeanor.

"Looks like she lifted this purse from a Sara Cohen," responded the officer.

"I ain't no thief!" yelled the woman indignantly. "My friend gave it to me to hold for her."

"Where is this friend?" inquired the officer sardonically.

"I don't know. You want me to do everything—hold the bag and know everything? I can't do everything," asserted the woman.

The officers led the woman, who was still clinging to the purse away from the platform.

Above ground, the moon brought raindrops to accompany him on his shift. Tiny, fragrant droplets provided a cooling balm over the restless city. Sara searched her pockets for her cell phone, but it was missing, as was her purse. She tried to retrace her steps, but she could not recall her whereabouts for the entire afternoon. The grass grew moist from the droplets of rain. Sara's clothing clung to her as she lay across a park bench in Washington Square Park. The persistent raindrops provided a moist blanket as she slept.

"Who is this?" asked Stephen as a voice on the other end of the phone spoke.

"A friend," answered the voice. "You'd better get over to Washington Square Park right away. It's dark; I don't think you want your girlfriend sleeping on a park bench in the dark."

Stephen heard the click of the receiver. He phoned the apartment. Sara's voice invited callers to leave messages. For some reason, the mysterious caller felt a sense of responsibility on Sara's behalf. The voice was unfamiliar. Stephen wondered why he was called and not Sara's parents. It occurred to him that Sara wanted him to find her and left only his phone number as a contact number.

Stephen approached the sleeping Sara guardedly, looking around for signs of onlookers, who might make both of them prey in the darkened park. The droplets turned hostile in the dark and splattered everything with oppressive moisture. Sara slept in her usual carefree manner. She wore no shoes and seemed to possess only the clothes on her back. As anticipated, the smell of alcohol inundated her presence. Stephen shook her gently and then more vigorously when she did not respond.

"What have I done to you?" groaned Stephen as he lifted her to a sitting position. The inimical rain thrust bullets upon them mercilessly. Stephen held Sara's wobbly head to his chest.

Tears and rain mingled together in a pathetic truce upon his face as he lifted her into his arms and carried her to the emergency room of New York University Hospital.

"Do you want me to wait until they come out?" asked the mysterious voice into his cell phone as he watched Stephen carry Sara into the emergency room. "I'm double-parked, but I can stay here, if you want."

"No," said Sheridon Southgate, "let the family take it from here. You've done enough. Keep an eye on the brother. He'll probably need help as well, but don't intercede without informing me. I want everything to go smoothly. Get the pictures to Cohen, and let him know that I interceded out of the goodness of my heart. He can show his gratitude by handing over the photos he plans to use against me."

"Done," said the voice. The black sedan drove away slowly into a stream of traffic.

Sheridon Southgate looked out of his penthouse window. The city sparkled and gleamed. It didn't bother him that he could not see any stars. The city lights were enough; in point-of-fact, he and the city lights were alike. They were artificial, but they controlled their own environments. They did not depend upon the light from the moon or the sun or the stars. They made their own light. More often than not, the light was so bright that it overpowered the heavenly lights, and it was to Sheridon's liking.

•   •   •

Jonathan rested on the sofa. He stared at nothing in particular, but he was aware of the hint of Sara's perfume on the sofa cushion. He wondered if Stephen and Sara been together on the sofa. It was a logical conclusion. His sister was not brazen enough to take a man to her bed immediately. Even Sara would not be that coarse. Jonathan stood up and took Mitzi from the corner. He made a mental note to remove the sofa from the apartment along with any trace of his sister and her lover. If she wanted Stephen, she could have him. Mitzi mourned as Jonathan's bow struck her strings fervently. The door opened. Stephen walked in and placed his keys on the dining area table.

"You're back," said Stephen walking slowly to the sofa.

"So it would appear," said Jonathan placing Mitzi back in the corner.

"Sara's in the hospital," said Stephen.

"I've heard," said Jonathan. "I must say, your caretaker skills leave much to be desired, Stephen. I leave you in charge and..."

"I can't do this right now," said Stephen. "I can't take a confrontation right now."

"Where have you been?" asked Jonathan. "Sara was admitted hours ago. Grandfather phoned around eight. It's almost midnight. Where have you been?"

"I've been walking around and thinking," said Stephen.

"Well, that's a first," said Jonathan. "How long has it been since you exercised that brain of yours to think?"

"I can't argue with you," said Stephen. "I don't have anything left. Say what you will. Do what you will. I can't fight you. I know that you and your family are upset."

"Well, that's an understatement," said Jonathan.

"I'll have all of my things out in the morning," said Stephen. "I hope that you won't let your grandfather shut down the programs. Those inner-city kids are depending on us, and all of the staff is depending on an income and a place to live until the fall semester begins. Please don't take your anger out on them."

Jonathan smiled. "What makes you think I'm angry, Stephen?"

"All right then, your revenge. I know you, Jonathan. You won't rest until I have paid for my mistake."

"Then you admit that it was a mistake?" asked Jonathan hopefully. "Your involvement with Sara was a mistake?"

"I didn't say that," said Stephen.

"Then what are you saying?" asked Jonathan bitterly. "What was your mistake?"

"I didn't handle things properly," said Stephen.

"You are a master of understatement," smirked Jonathan. "Don't you realize what you've done to this family? We have all invested in you, and what do you do? You throw it into our faces."

Jonathan's words struck a chord within Stephen's heart. Suddenly, he felt his strength return. "You have all invested in me?" asked Stephen. "I was some sort of investment?" Stephen smiled and stood up. "All of this time, I have been beating up on myself for hurting you and Sara, when all along, I was nothing more than some type of experiment or investment."

"It wasn't like that," amended Jonathan. "My words were careless."

"No," said Stephen, "your words were precise and truthful. It was a Freudian slip, but it was the truth, nonetheless. I was a charity case – a poor student that your family would help. I was a social experiment for you and Sara. No, I'm not in your league, but I don't want to be. I can't believe that I've been blaming myself."

"Where are you going?" asked Jonathan.

"I don't know," answered Stephen. "I have to get out of here."

"Not before we settle things," said Jonathan.

"Things are settled," said Stephen. "I am out of the apartment, out of the corporation, and out of your lives. Sara is in the hospital, where she'll finally get the help she needs."

"They can't give her the help she needs, Stephen," said Jonathan. "Please, sit down. There are other factors."

"What factors?" asked Stephen. "They can help her, can't they?"

"My grandfather is placing Sara in a rehabilitation center in Arizona," said Jonathan.

"Arizona? Why is he sending her all the way to Arizona?" asked Stephen.

"The best facility in the country is located in Phoenix. Of course, Grandfather wants the best for Sara."

"That's understandable," said Stephen. "How long will she have to stay? She'll be able to start fall semester, won't she?"

"Sara's pregnant, Stephen," said Jonathan matter-of-factly.

"She can't be pregnant," said Stephen. "It isn't possible."

"The hospital tests beg to differ," said Jonathan. "So, you see, you are a part of the family. You are not an experiment or an investment. You are a valued part of the family. You are going to be a father, and I am going to be an uncle."

"Have you lost your mind?" asked Stephen. "Sara is not prepared to be a mother any more than I am prepared to be a father!" yelled Stephen.

"Well," said Jonathan thoughtfully, "this is what happens when you align yourself with someone with a uterus."

"This can't be happening," said Stephen closing his eyes and breathing rapidly.

"There is a solution," said Jonathan, "apart from the unseemly termination of the pregnancy."

Stephen looked up. "What is it?"

"As you recall, during one of our moments of passion, we entertained the thought of adopting a child. Do you remember?" asked Jonathan.

"Don't do this, Jonathan," said Stephen.

"You made a commitment, and I'm holding you to it," said Jonathan.

"You're insane," asserted Stephen. "How can you think of that now?"

"This is the best time," reasoned Jonathan. "Don't you see? It makes perfect sense. Sara has the baby, preferably out in Arizona, and I will adopt it. I can rear it in New Haven. Don't you see? You and Sara can be together, and I will always have a part of you. We will always be together."

Stephen stood up again. "I am still the investment, aren't I? I am still an object, and you will never stop trying to figure out ways to use me."

Jonathan laughed. "Use you? How have I used you? It was not my idea for you to impregnate my sister. I am not using you. I am trying to help you."

"You are trying to help yourself!" yelled Stephen. "You want to imprison me and to keep me manacled to you for the rest of my life. You would even be willing to use an innocent child to do it. No thanks. I don't want any part of it, and I don't want any part of you. It's over, Jonathan. I didn't have the courage to tell you before, but you've given me the courage to tell you now. It is over, and I don't ever want to see you again." Stephen walked to the dining area table and picked up his keys. Jonathan laughed.

"You think that you can walk away from me, but you are wrong," assured Jonathan. "I will always be a part of your life, Stephen; you will never be free of me."

"Go to hell," said Stephen as he walked out of the door and slammed it.

"Pack your bags, Stephen," laughed Jonathan, "for you'll be going with me."

Chapter IXX

The gushing waters of the pond gurgled and cascaded into a diminutive waterfall. Winston leaned his head against the bark of the elm tree, which provided shade and a sense of security. The waters soothed his frazzled nerves. Birds chirped gaily, and ducks floated with careless ease upon the glassy surface of the pond. Winston threw a pebble into the water and watched the ripples enervate the water. The spires of the high school peeked over the branches at the top of the elm tree. During the summer, it was difficult to see the high school through the foliage, but the majestic spires refused to be consumed by a few paltry trees. They were regal and knew their rightful place as overseers of the lush expanse. A few ducks quacked vociferously in protest of the quivering effects the intrusive pebbles made upon the sedated pond. Winston smiled mischievously.

"It's not like you to be mean-spirited," said a voice behind him.

"Pull up a rock and sit down," said Winston.

Arnold sat next to his friend, and they enjoyed the relaxing environs for a few moments without speaking. "Did you bring the Gatorade?" asked Arnold.

"I did not," said Winston. "You know that you are not supposed to drink it. Here, I brought bottled water." Winston took a bottle of Evian water out of a plastic bag and gave it to his friend.

"What are you my doctor now?" asked Arnold. He took the water, opened it, and drank a few sips. "This is nice and cold. Thanks."

"You are welcome," said Winston.

"The old place still feels like home," said Arnold wistfully. "Look up. You can see the old spires surveying everything in its purview." They both looked up for a few moments and smiled.

"I used to think that those points on the tower were following me," said Winston. "Everywhere I went, they were there watching, guiding, and judging. 'Did you do your homework? Do you really have time to play ball? Is that language appropriate?' I always felt that I was being challenged to grow, achieve, and make something of myself."

"That's why we still come here," responded Arnold.

"So, why did you want to meet me here?" asked Winston.

"How are things going on the eighty-second floor? How is the computer program working out?"

"Without it, I tell you, I don't know what I would do. Sheridon is planning to take Guy to England. I can't stop him. I suppose Guy deserves a real family."

"You are his real family," advised Arnold.

"Sheridon can give him much more, and now that I've met Taylor and Kate, how can I deny Guy the chance to live and grow with them? You ask about the program? I would be at the end of my rope without Stephen and the guys up there."

"I fired Lawrence today," said Arnold remorsefully.

Winston stared at his friend. "What are you talking about? You can't fire Stephen. He keeps that program running. Without Stephen, there *is* no program."

"I had no choice," said Arnold. "Sara is in the hospital. She passed out on a subway after drinking herself into a stupor. Lawrence has been involved with both Sara and Jonathan."

Winston closed his eyes and leaned against the elm tree. "What are you saying?"

"You know perfectly well what I'm saying," said Arnold. "You wouldn't happen to have anything stronger in that plastic bag of yours, would you?"

"I had no idea. How is she?" asked Winston.

"I'm sending her to a rehabilitation center in Arizona. She will be able to recuperate while I plan the next step."

"What next step?" asked Winston.

"Sara is pregnant," said Arnold without feeling.

Winston sat upright. "She's just a kid! Why did she go and do a thing like that? I take it Stephen is responsible?"

"Lawrence ended the relationship with Sara yesterday, and she tried to drink herself into oblivion. He ended it with Jonathan too, but it's too late. The harm has been done," said Arnold.

"What do Daniel and Elizabeth say about all of this?" asked Winston.

"They don't know anything. I wouldn't trust those two feebleminded morons with something as serious as this. The matter will be handled with discretion, and Sara will be free to proceed with her plans to enter the university in the fall." Arnold looked upward at the spires, which seemed to be scowling downward in the late afternoon sun.

"You are not suggesting..."

"There is no alternative," said Arnold. "Sara is too young to assume the responsibility of a baby, and Jonathan would never reconcile such a birth. It would destroy him."

"Surely, you can't make a decision like this without thinking of the child," pleaded Winston.

"I *am* thinking of the child," said Arnold. "Believe me, it will be the best thing. Sara would only miss the first two weeks or so of the fall semester, then things will be back to normal."

"You're missing the point. Sara could put it up for adoption," insisted Winston.

"Winston, you never change," said Arnold. "I appreciate that your heart is in the right place, but you must understand that there are no easy solutions in 2001. Your well-intentioned proposal is, most assuredly, out of the question."

The two friends sat silently on the bank and gazed into the placid water.

"What have you got there?" asked a young Winston waiting for his jubilant friend, Arnold, to supply the breadcrumbs from his book bag to feed the ducks.

"It's the test for Mr. Gralen's class tomorrow. The old geezer left a copy of it on the desk in the library. Harold Xeroxed copies for everyone. We'll all get 'A's. Harvard, here we come!" exclaimed Arnold. The expression on his friend's dour face dampened Arnold's enthusiasm.

"You can't keep it," proclaimed Winston. "Give it back."

"Are you stupid? "asked Arnold. "This is the test. We can get A's."

"I plan to get an 'A,'" said Winston, "but not by cheating."

"Everyone has the test by now," said Arnold. "If we don't use it, we'll fail."

"Not if I tell Mr. Gralen," said Winston.

"Who are you, Joan of Arc, or something?" asked Arnold. "I thought that we were friends."

"We *are* friends," said Winston, "and I'm going to tell Mr. Gralen so that he can give us a different test."

"I almost hate you, Winston!" shrieked Arnold as he tore the test into small pieces and scattered them across the pond. He stormed away.

"You don't hate me," uttered Winston to himself smiling as his friend vanished into a crowd of students walking across the verdant campus. "You told me so that I would stop you, just like a real friend would do."

The clear, afternoon sky turned into a tranquil, orange haze. Dusk soon glazed the mosaic landscape. The spires settled down to rest, and the two friends in the autumn of their years, sat in silence feeling the onset of winter's chill in the midst of summer.

"It's getting late," said Arnold. "I'd better be on my way." He stood up and looked above the trees. The spires were ensconced in the tangerine glow of dusk.

"You can't fire Stephen," said Winston looking at the tranquil lake. "We need him up there. And with regard to Sara..."

Arnold placed his hand on his friend's shoulder. "I wish I didn't have to, my friend. Let's have lunch this week. Let Simmons know when you'll be free." Arnold walked away quietly. Winston gazed at the pond as darkness descended around him.

●   ●   ●

The warm afternoon sun provided a lavish feast for the vivid array of flowers in the garden. Sara watched a bee flounce from flower to flower. Summer in Phoenix was less celebratory than summer in New York. Sara missed the throbbing energy of the city and the aroma of foods sizzling on the street vendors' carts. Everything inside of the rehabilitation center was subdued, but outside in the garden, the intoxicating fragrance of effervescent flowers jolted Sara's senses. Indoors, her five senses were lethargic and barren. The child growing within her womb would, surely, be the dullest creature; what's more, Sara remained uncertain of the embryo's fate. It was an anomaly - a freak of nature, as it were. Genetically, there was no precedent. Although the embryo was carefully monitored, Sara felt that it was an interloper traversing the boundaries of civilization. Be that as it may, Sara reasoned that the world harbored countless interlopers—unwelcome, unloved, and utterly intrusive. The child would not suffer loss of any kind. It would be loved and provided with all of the accoutrements of a privileged life. What troubled Sara was the feeling of alienation that seemed to penetrate her being. The embryo was no longer a semblance of the love she shared with Stephen; it was now the future source of healing for Jonathan and an indefatigable source of cells to restore health to her brother's deteriorating body. A gentle hand touched Sara's hair. Sara looked up into her brother's eyes.

"You've cut your hair," observed Jonathan as he sat beside his sister on a bench in the garden. "How are they treating you?"

"I'm not sure that I can go through with this, Jonathan. I don't think that we thought it through."

"I know that this is difficult," comforted Jonathan, "but it will be over soon, and you and Stephen can begin anew."

Sara shuddered. "Why won't they let him visit me? How am I supposed to handle this alone?"

"I have a surprise for you," smiled Jonathan. Sara searched her brother's eyes. Their shimmering radiance provided a sense of solace and reassurance. "I brought a surprise for you," continued Jonathan. His crystalline gaze focused upon the door to the lounge, where Stephen Lawrence stood inside of the portal. "Remember," whispered Jonathan, "No one must know of our secret." Jonathan took his leave as Stephen advanced through the invisible gate into the womb of the garden. Stephen's eyes seemed weary and betrayed the full extent of the stressful circumstance.

"Your hair looks lovely," said Stephen holding Sara's frigid hands within his. She seemed so young and fragile in the white hospital gown. "How are you feeling?"

"I'm confused," said Sara clutching Stephen's warm hands.

"That is to be expected. This is a difficult dilemma for anyone to handle," reassured Stephen, "but we'll get through it."

Sara could not look into Stephen's eyes. "I'm afraid," said Sara at last.

"It will be over soon. We need to begin looking for a home for the baby. There are quite a few reputable adoption agencies right here in Phoenix," said Stephen.

Sara's hands trembled. Stephen held them tightly. "I know that this is a lot to think about, but we can place the baby in a loving home here in Phoenix, and then you will be able to return to New York and begin your freshman year during the spring semester. All of this trouble will be far behind us." Stephen held Sara closely. He could feel her tremulous heart. "You're shaking. Tell me what you're thinking," said Stephen.

"I think that Sara has had enough today," said Jonathan joining the pair with a nurse. "Why don't you go inside and rest awhile, Sara?"

Buoyed by her brother's reassuring gaze, Sara stood and walked slowly through the lounge door with the nurse.

"Where are you going?" called Stephen after her. "We must talk about this. There are decisions to be made. Sara, come back!" The lounge door closed slowly. "What have you done to her?" demanded Stephen.

"What have *I* done?" asked Jonathan. "Please, sit down, Stephen. You are right. There is much to discuss."

Stephen looked at Jonathan angrily. "I have no intention of discussing anything with you. Do not try to interfere, Jonathan."

"The child concerns all of us, Stephen," said Jonathan smugly.

Stephen became incensed. "The entire world revolves around you, doesn't it? Why must everything promote Jonathan's wants, desires, and sense of privilege?"

Jonathan sat calmly on the bench taking in the colorful, fragrant ambiance. His winsome gaze settled upon a giddy, blue flower with gentle petals. "The mind of man is fashioned and built up, even as a strain of music," recited Jonathan absentmindedly.

"What?" asked Stephen distractedly looking towards the lounge door and hoping that Sara would re-emerge.

"I believe," continued Jonathan, "that there are spirits, which when they form a favoured being from his very dawn of infancy, do open out of the clouds..." A soft, shimmering gleam of crystal light penetrated Jonathan's gaze.

"What are you babbling about?" demanded Stephen impatiently.

Jonathan's irrepressible gaze fixed upon Stephen.

"I *am* that favoured being," said Jonathan. "It is only fitting that the child brings health and pleasure to me and to my family." Stephen was incredulous.

"Your selfishness is beyond belief," uttered Stephen with disgust.

"I, too, am a part of the child Sara bears. I, too, will be its father," said Jonathan.

"You've grown mad!" retorted Stephen. "You will never adopt this child, Jonathan. I am going to find Sara. Stay out of our lives."

"I cannot," said Jonathan. "I am an inextricable part of the child and of you. I told you that we would never be separated, but you were dubious. Now, you see how everything falls into place."

"You are out of your mind," said Stephen starting for the lounge door.

"The laws of nature are skewed in our favor, Stephen. We will change modern medicine forever," said Jonathan confidently. Stephen stopped abruptly.

"What did you say?" inquired Stephen as he remembered the first time that he heard the arrogant proclamation. Stephen's head began to throb and his heart beat frantically. "What have you done?" wailed Stephen. Before Jonathan could respond, Stephen charged towards him like an incensed bull. He grabbed Jonathan and shook him violently. "What have you done?" screamed Stephen.

"I have ensured our future together," answered the favourite being as he removed himself from Stephen's grasp and walked calmly into the lounge to join his sister. Stephen crumbled onto the bench, and the Edenic Garden turned miasmic.

• • •

Stephen walked purposefully into his office in order to collect his belongings. Neglected papers covered his desk in his absence. The office was empty and still. An orange twilight covered the New York skyline as a somber darkness descended. The intern's head continued to throb as his world collapsed around him. The room began to spin as he sat in the cushioned chair. Visions of Sara and Jonathan constellated around corporate contracts, dollar bills, and voracious eagles laughing absurdly on the face of the currency. Stephen closed his eyes as the distorted eagles encircled him. Their cruel, sinister eyes bulged, and their shrill laughter created a discordant ring in Stephen's ears. One eagle, massive and majestic, hovered above the others and watched as the hideous, winged creatures emptied the contents of Stephen's briefcase. Papers swirled through the air. The malevolent fiends stripped Stephen's clothing from his body and pulled his hair with their treacherous beaks. The large, regal bird swooped down with tremendous speed and clutched Stephen's ankles with his formidable talons. The terrified young man released a horrified gasp as he ascended helplessly. The powerful grasp of the eagle's wing covered his chest, and its gripping talons became a vice around his ankles. Stephen's heart beat furiously and his forehead was covered with beads of perspiration. Through his peripheral vision, Stephen glimpsed the sketch of Michelangelo's *Ganymede*, which, somehow, had reappeared on the wall opposite his desk. The beautiful Trojan prince smirked at the lowly intern. Stephen hurled a metal paper weight at the picture. Through shards of broken glass on the floor, Ganymede smiled victoriously. Stephen slumped into a deathlike slumber onto his desk as the neglected papers provided a mocking, tortuous pillow.

•   •   •

Winston Brielle was the last to enter the chauffer-driven grey SUV. James, Arnold Cohen's chauffer, drove expeditiously through the morning rush-hour traffic.

Nigel, Phillip, and seven of the Summer Initiatives staff chatted amiably in preparation for the first meeting with the inner-city students. Winston briefed them on the types of behaviors they might encounter, but the briefing did not deter the optimism and enthusiasm that filled the SUV. Noticeably missing were the two program heads – Jonathan and Stephen. Winston felt that their absence was a vote of confidence in his ability to handle the Computers-in-Schools Program. He knew that this first solo outing was his opportunity to spread his wings, so to speak, to demonstrate his many abilities and show Arnold, Jonathan, and Stephen that he was worthy of their trust.

Winston checked his pocket to make certain that his heart medication was close at hand. As a retired principal, he was well-acquainted with the attitudes and recalcitrant behaviors of many inner-city students, and he was prepared for any contingency. Upon his insistence, the staff shed their informal summer attire of polo shirts, khaki Bermuda shorts, and sandals for dark suits with crisp Oxford pin-striped shirts, conservative ties, and leather shoes. Winston went so far as to wear a handkerchief that matched his tie. It was important to set the proper example of office attire. There would be no tee shirts, sneakers, jeans, headphones, visible tattoos or body piercings allowed at any of the meetings. The students would be expected to report to the office wearing appropriate business attire. A stipend was given to the school for student clothing expenses. After weeks of preparation, Winston and his staff would finally meet their charges. The air was charged with the vibrant electricity that accompanies new beginnings.

The students sat listlessly in the dark, drab auditorium. A faded American flag and frayed navy blue velveteen curtains bedecked the stage. Winston's voice filled the auditorium. The Computers-in-Schools staff distributed pamphlets about the program. One hand was raised in the stuffy auditorium. Winston called upon the rather thin, tall girl with large, hollow eyes and tawny braided hair extensions that descended down her back. The girl stood confidently. Her voice was abrasive and gruff. It did not seem to fit her body.

"Somebody said that we gettin' free Nikes. I just want to know which ones we gettin.' I already got the suede ones. Which ones we gettin' for being in this program?"

Winston breathed deeply to conceal his irritation. "First of all, the sneakers are not being awarded for participation in the program. Hopefully, you are here because you are interested in computers. I am certain that the Nike Corporation will contribute a wide array of sneakers. Heaven forbid that any of you should receive last year's model," said Winston. He heard his remark as he spoke, but he could not contain the sarcasm. It flowed out of him like a purging riptide. The dilapidated setting and the surly attitudes of the inner-city children were reminiscent of his experiences trying to help those who seemed bent on destroying all of the values he and others like him tried to impart. Winston changed his tone and expression. Before he could speak, the young woman began her tirade. She stood quickly and placed her hands on her under-formed hips.

"You don't have to get smart!" blurted the girl. Her voice became deep and filled with friction. "I just *axed* a question." The girl stared at Winston with menacing eyes that shot vipers at him. Nigel joined Winston at the podium.

"May I?" asked Nigel.

"Be my guest," uttered Winston. He stepped aside and let Nigel man the podium.

Nigel calmed the pending student eruption in a calm, rational manner. He spoke to the students in a straight-forward manner, not the least bit condescending. They listened to him. Nigel's voice quelled the tension in the emotionally-charged air. For the first time, Winston saw the young man as a skillful mediator and felt ashamed at his own lack of patience and encouragement. When Nigel finished speaking, Winston resumed his place at the podium.

The combatant girl stood again. "See, he know how to talk to people. You just rude."

Winston remained calm. "What is your name?" asked Winston politely.

"My name is Darlene. What's your name?" demanded the girl. Winston did not answer. "I know you goin' to kick me out of the program. I don't care. I don't need no sneakers. I got sneakers." The young irritant maneuvered herself out of her seat and into the aisle. Her approach to the auditorium's rear door was halted by an imposing figure blocking the exit. The principal stood like a drill sergeant guarding the door. Her limbs were heavy, and her form was rectangular. The woman's thin hair was exceedingly short and plastered across her head to her ears. Her smile was treacherous. Darlene quickly climbed over the students and returned to her seat. The principal strode to the front of the auditorium.

"I think that Darlene would like to apologize for her unfortunate behavior," said the principal. Her eyes exploded with shrapnel that filtered through every crevice of the auditorium. Darlene's gaze lingered downward to avoid impact.

"Sorry," said the fallen soldier.

"Now, if anyone else has anything to say, say it now," ordered the militaristic principal. The auditorium remained hushed. The principal turned to Winston.

"I am sorry that I am late, Mr. Brielle. We had a minor problem in the office that needed my attention. Please continue your presentation. I don't think that there will be any further disturbances."

"Thank you, Ms. Irving," said Winston. "I would like to introduce some of the members of The Computers-in-Schools Programs. They will be working closely with you through August, at which time they will return to their respective colleges and universities. The second phase of our program will begin in September with a new staff and first-hand experiences within our corporate office. Some of you will be selected for internship positions; in addition, there may be scholarship money available for those of you who plan to graduate next year and are accepted into accredited colleges or universities." The students looked at Winston incredulously. A student in the front row raised his hand. He stood when Winston called upon him and seemed out of place within the group. In the sea of tee shirts, jeans, and sneakers, the young man wore a blue Oxford pin-striped shirt, navy pants, and loafers, and his impeccable diction caused

Winston to gaze at him in wonder. "I am sorry," said Winston, "would you repeat your question?"

"Certainly," said the young man with assurance. "I inquired as to whether the program would offer tutoring to help us prepare for the SATs. Some of us will take it for the first time, and we have not had sufficient preparation."

"What is your name," asked Winston.

"My name is Thomas Grant, Mr. Brielle," answered the young man, "and I really appreciate this opportunity."

"Hey, Grant," yelled an anonymous voice from the auditorium, "why don't you take off your camisole and fight like a man?" The audience roared with laughter. Mrs. Irving stood and surveyed each side of the room. Silence ensued when her eyes met each row. Thomas Grant sat quietly.

"I am certain that we will be able to provide some type of SAT preparation," assured Winston. "Our program is all-inclusive; we would like to prepare you for long-term and short-term success. One of the leading manufacturers in New York is contributing the business attire you need for the workplace. There will be etiquette coaches to help you dress, speak, and conduct yourselves in the workplace environment. These experiences will be invaluable to your future success. The pamphlets you are now receiving have timelines and schedules for all events and training sessions. Please note that there will be a getting acquainted picnic in Central Park in August and a formal celebration to begin the program in September. We look forward to working with you, and we thank you for your cooperation and participation."

The students filed out of the auditorium slowly and orderly under the watchful eye of Ms. Irving. The visit provided Winston with the adrenaline needed to gain focus and momentum. For the first time in many months, he felt a surge of commitment and dedication to under-represented inner-city youth. It was a good feeling.

• • •

Stephen sat anxiously in the waiting room. He noticed his pale, thin hands, which were in need of a manicure. His suit hung uncomfortably upon his thin shoulders. Stephen guessed that he had lost seven or eight pounds. He had neither eaten nor slept since he saw Sara, and he had not discussed his dilemma with anyone. He considered going home to New Jersey to discuss the matter with his parish priest, but he was too ashamed to go to confession. He knew that his thoughts were wrong, but he could not think of any way out of the troublous circumstance. The young, attractive receptionist gazed at Stephen with interest. Something about Stephen's vulnerable demeanor attracted women and men alike, but the last thing he needed was another female looking at him adoringly.

"Mr. Southgate will see you now," said the comely young woman. Her welcoming smile exposed glowing, white teeth. Stephen stood conscious of his ill-fitting suit.

"Thank you," said Stephen quietly.

The receptionist led Stephen through a long hallway with royal blue, plush carpeting. Stephen tried to remember the office the last time he visited. He did not recall the carpeting, and the walk to Sheridon's office seemed shorter on the first visit. Clearly, the suite of offices had been remodeled. The receptionist opened a large, oak door with a circular golden handle. Sheridon Southgate sat comfortably behind a massive desk. He stood smiling when Stephen entered and greeted him with a hearty handshake.

"Mr. Lawrence, do come in and have a seat." Sheridon gestured to a plush, grey leather sofa that was, quite possibly, the largest sofa Stephen had ever seen. It encircled the entire office and provided seating from any direction. The New York skyline glistened through clear, crystalline windows that surrounded the office. Stephen could not see his shoes in the grey carpeting.

It was much thicker than the royal blue affair that bedecked the hallway.

"Well, what do you think?" asked Sheridon looking around the room. Truly, Stephen had never seen such opulence.

"Impressive," said Stephen.

"It's lavish," said Sheridon. "Perhaps you will consider coming to work for me when your internship concludes with Cohen Enterprises in September."

"How do you know when my internship concludes?" asked Stephen.

Sheridon sat beside Stephen on the supple gray leather sofa. "The first thing to learn about the business world, Mr. Lawrence, is to do your homework. I know everything about you. I know that you are a man who likes to reason, and I estimated that it would take three weeks or so before you would come to pay me a visit." Sheridon took a cigar from a porcelain tray on an expansive, glass coffee table. "I know that you don't smoke, but do you mind if I light up?" asked Sheridon.

"I would rather you didn't," said Stephen dryly.

Sheridon returned the cigar to the tray. "Very well, would you like to tell me why you are here, or would you rather I tell you?"

"Why don't you tell me," said Stephen. "You seem to be omniscient."

"You want me to authorize an abortion for Sara at my facility, an accidental *mishap*, shall we say. Neither the venerable Arnold Cohen nor the debonair Jonathan Cohen will agree, and you do not want to summon her parents from Portugal with such garish news. I seem to be your only hope. I must say, Mr. Lawrence, I commend your sacrifice and courage. You are vehemently opposed to abortion and ending a human life, as it were. Your decision is eating you alive. You cannot eat, and you cannot sleep. You are losing weight, and you are unable to think clearly or to make decisions with your usual adroitness. Am I correct?"

"It isn't a human being. It is some ungodly creature," uttered Stephen.

"I beg to differ," said Sheridon. He walked to his desk and retrieved a brown manila envelope. From the envelope, he produced a picture and placed it on the elegant table before Stephen. "This is a picture of your son," said Sheridon. "Those little protrusions are his genitals." Stephen could not remove his eyes from the image. "Your son is a human being. Look at his little fingers beginning to form. Look at his toes. He is alive and well. You and Sara have a son."

Stephen lifted the image from the table and viewed it carefully. "You're forgetting something, aren't you?" Stephen threw the image at Sheridon. "I *know* what you did!" yelled Stephen. "This isn't a baby. It's a freak—a monster!"

"Easy, Mr. Lawrence," said Sheridon. "Let me get you a glass of wine or perhaps something stronger. Sheridon poured a drink from a crystal decanter into a small glass and handed it to Stephen. Stephen drank it quickly without noticing whether it was wine or whiskey. He placed the glass on the table. Sheridon refilled it.

"Let's be rational, Mr. Lawrence," said Sheridon. "The child is growing normally. That is no small feat considering how much alcohol Sara ingested before she was admitted into the rehabilitation center. We do not know the extent of the damage to the embryo yet, and we may not know for quite some time, but look at him, Stephen. He is growing perfectly. The little fellow has the spirit to thrive, just like his father."

"Which father?" asked Stephen sardonically. "Jonathan is Sara's brother. There's no getting around that. Yes, I have a son…but you've implanted Jonathan's cells within the embryo as well. Don't tell me that the child won't suffer any consequences." Stephen poured himself another glass of the brown liquid and drank it quickly.

"There is relevance to what you say," said Sheridon sipping his drink calmly, "but think of it as a transplant. People receive organ transplants from relatives, do they not? Yes, Jonathan is a part of the child, but as Sara's brother, he is genetically linked to the child from the outset. There is truth to what I say."

"There is incest to what you say!" yelled Stephen. He poured himself another drink and swallowed it quickly.

"Come now, Mr. Lawrence," said Sheridon, "Let's be honest with one another. You are less concerned about the child's relation to Sara and Jonathan than you are to the child's relation to you and Jonathan. With my procedure, you and Jonathan have a child. The fact that Sara is Jonathan's sister is a complication, but think of the future. If this procedure is effective, it opens the door for men like Jonathan and yourself to actually have a child together. Don't you know what this means? The market for this technology will be unparalleled. We will make a fortune!" proclaimed Sheridon with glee. Stephen rose from the sofa, grabbed the crystal decanter, and hurled it at Sheridon's head. Sheridon ducked. The decanter shattered against the wall leaving a brown stain on the eggshell finish. Immediately, the door opened. Three security guards in plain clothing entered and apprehended the wobbly, incoherent intern.

"Leave him alone," said Sheridon. "I'll handle this." The men nodded and exited the office. "Sit down, Stephen, please," said Sheridon calmly. "I know that you are upset, but violence is beneath you."

Stephen breathed deeply. His senses were clouded, his vision was blurred, and he could not find the words to speak. Sheridon opened his desk draw and turned on a recorder. Stephen heard a thumping noise. "This is the heartbeat of your son, Mr. Lawrence," said Sheridon as he amplified the volume. The sound of the heartbeat grew louder and stronger in stereophonic sound, which surrounded the room. Stephen placed his hands to his ears. "Turn it off!" yelled Stephen.

"You would like to abort the child," said Sheridon loudly over the sound of the heartbeat, "but you realize that it *is* a child with all of the parts of a human being. You have seen your son, Stephen, and now you can hear his heart beating. To end his life would be nothing short of murder."

The heartbeat continued to throb in Stephen's ears. "Please, turn it off," pleaded Stephen. He collapsed upon the sofa whimpering helplessly.

Sheridon turned off the recorder. "I cannot take a human life, Mr. Lawrence," said Sheridon. "I do not believe that you can either." Sheridon sat beside the cringing intern. "Go home and get some rest, Mr. Lawrence. This is not the tragedy you imagine. Look on the bright side. Perhaps with a child to care for, Sara will preserve her own life. Jonathan will be able to live a normal life, thanks to this procedure, and you, Mr. Lawrence, will be a part of the two people you love. Go home and think of the positive outcomes. I apologize for the harshness of my methods today, but I think that you understand how important your cooperation and confidentiality are in this matter. If the media finds out about this, I will be destroyed, yes, but so will you, Jonathan, Sara, and the child. Your pictures will be plastered on the front of every scandal sheet in America and abroad. Your son will be treated as a freak of nature and subject to medical inquiry. The Cohen empire will crumble. Jonathan has convinced his grandfather that a great-grandson to carry on the Cohen dynasty is something to be desired. Knowledge of the procedure will kill him. I do not want that to happen, Stephen, do you? Go home and get some rest. Things will look better in the morning. In fact, why don't you take a vacation—my treat, of course. My father is handling the computer program with your able staff. You've worked hard to get the program up and running. Take some time off. My jet is at your disposal. You name the place, and I will handle all of the arrangements. When you return, you will be refreshed and better able to handle all of this. You need time away from everything." Sheridon shook Stephen gently. "Poor kid, you missed my eloquent speech, didn't you?" Sheridon walked to his desk and pressed a button. His winsome receptionist appeared in the doorway. "April, get Errol," said Sheridon.

"Yes, Mr. Southgate," said the young woman cheerfully. A tall, handsome young man with sandy hair and gentle green eyes appeared in the doorway with the receptionist.

"Summon a cab, and both of you accompany Mr. Lawrence to his apartment to help him pack. He's a little tipsy from the alcohol. I'm sending all of you on a short vacation. Do what you can to see that Mr. Lawrence is happy and rested. If anyone asks any questions at his residence, tell them that you are old friends from college and that he's spending a few days with you. Don't mention my name or the corporation, and take his cell phone. Oh yes, there is a dog at the residence. I believe his name is Freemont. With Jonathan in Brazil for the week, people will become suspicious if Stephen leaves without him. I suppose you'll have to take the dog with you."

"I'm allegoric to dogs," replied Errol calmly. "Perhaps we can put him in a kennel."

"Take an allergy pill," said Sheridon impatiently. "The dog will accompany you."

"Yes, Mr. Southgate," said Errol sorrowfully.

"Thank you, Mr. Southgate," said April as she and Errol helped Stephen to his feet. Stephen walked shakily out of the office with their help incognizant of what was happening. Sheridon Southgate sat on his plush, gray sofa away from the broken crystal decanter on the carpet. He lit a cigar and sat back smiling. Life was a wondrous affair. The merger with Bentley Wireless went through without hindrance, thanks to

Arnold Cohen's tumultuous family problems, which kept him distracted and occupied; as a result, Sheridon attained more wealth than he ever imagined. Yes, life was glorious, and with the new procedure on the horizon, there would be no end to his ability to accrue massive fortunes. It was a win-win situation, and Sheridon Southgate could do nothing less than win. Dear Reader, sometimes in order to win, one must lose, and the loss can be catastrophic.

Chapter XX

Finding himself outstretched on a stripped chaise lounge, Stephen Lawrence awoke from a peaceful sleep and surveyed his surroundings. He observed the waves splashing against the calm, tranquil shore. The sudsy foam sizzled as it receded back into the contented, aqua sea. He was wearing a green floral short, snug maroon swimming trunks, and a straw hat with a green, floral band. Was this a dream? The sun messaged his skin and penetrated his body. The last thing he remembered was walking out of Sheridon Southgate's office assisted by a young man and a young woman. Freemont, stretched out on a blanket under a small umbrella next to the chaise lounge, climbed onto Stephen's lap and licked his chin.

"Hey, boy, what are you doing here?" asked Stephen elated to see a familiar friend. The young man who assisted him out of Sheridon's office appeared wearing blue trunks that revealed an elegant, well-maintained, slender body.

"You're awake," said Errol wiping the sea from his glistening body with a thick, white terrycloth towel. He threw the towel upon the sand and sat upon it. "Want to go for a swim?"

"Who are you?" asked Stephen trying to remember the young man's name.

"I'm Errol. We met in Mr. Southgate's office - remember?"

"Where are we, Errol?" asked Stephen. "How did I get here?"

"You are a guest of Mr. Southgate's," said Errol. "I cannot disclose the location at this time, but you will be well-cared for until Mr. Southgate sends his plane for us."

Stephen looked around. The beach seemed to be an island. A large, white house with colorful flora surrounding it stood majestically in the background. A smiling waiter in a formal white jacket and black pants appeared and left two fresh daiquiris on the side table. Stephen hoped that the waiter would speak and give an indication of accent, but the smiling waiter left and returned to the house without speaking. Errol sipped one of the daiquiris and lay on the beach towel.

"Am I a prisoner?" asked Stephen.

Errol laughed heartily. "That's funny, Stephen. Mr. Southgate's guests are pampered. Most don't want to leave when the plane comes."

"If I am here against my will, then I am nothing more than a prisoner," said Stephen calmly sipping the daiquiri. It was superb. "How long have I been here?"

"We arrived yesterday," replied Errol. "You were a tad worn from the alcohol you consumed in Mr. Southgate's office. "

"As I recall, I didn't drink that much alcohol," said Stephen, "certainly not enough to lose consciousness." The recollection of whiskey oozing down the wall of Sheridon's office jarred his memory, and he remembered hurling a bottle or a glass at Sheridon. Stephen surmised that something was in the whiskey that would render him semi-conscious. He returned the daiquiri to the side table suspiciously. "Are we the only ones here?" asked Stephen.

"April is here also. You won't be lonely, Stephen, we will see to that," said Errol.

Stephen checked his watch. "It is 2AM in New York. Since the sun is shining here, I assume that we have crossed the prime meridian." Errol remained silent as the sun glistened over his body. "How far are we from the United States?" asked Stephen. Errol did not speak. "You can't keep me here. I have responsibilities. People will wonder where I am. How did you get Freemont out of the apartment without anyone questioning you?"

"You are taking a brief vacation with friends, Stephen," said Errol without opening his eyes. "Everyone agreed that you needed a vacation. Jonathan convinced them. Don't worry, you will return in time for the grand celebration of the Computers-in-Schools program. Winston Brielle is leading your able team, and they are doing a magnificent job. Jonathan is taking charge of the overall operations. All is well, I assure you."

Jonathan's name sent an uncomfortable jolt through Stephen's body. "What role does Jonathan play in this ploy to keep me isolated?" Errol did not speak. "Jonathan arranged this, didn't he? He and Southgate are colluding together to separate me from Sara. It's true, isn't it?" Errol's silence, in Stephen's estimation, was an affirmation. "They won't get away with it," resolved Stephen. He shook his head in dismay. April appeared on the other side of the chaise lounge wearing a yellow-stripped bikini. Her sandy, tousled hair covered her shoulders. Stephen did not recall her hair reaching such proportions in the office; in point of fact, her hair was tightly arranged into a bun that exposed nothing more than her face.

"Hello, Stephen," said April. "May I get you anything?"

April looked remarkably similar to Sara. Stephen reasoned that the resemblance was a part of the unconscionable ploy. "No thank you," said Stephen with annoyance.

"All right," said April. "If you'd like to tour the island later, just let me know. I'm going for a swim." April ran into the festive surf. Stephen watched the waves play in her hair.

"I think that I would like to go inside now," said Stephen. "I imagine you have relieved me of my cell phone."

"I'm afraid so," said Errol sitting up smiling, "but we have a theater room with all of the latest movies, big-screen TV..."

"Computers?" asked Stephen.

"There is no Internet access here, Stephen," said Errol, "but we have an excellent chef. You will be happy here. Come, I'll take you on a tour of the house. There's a state-of-the-art fitness room with a personal trainer, yoga, you name it."

Stephen followed Errol into the house looking for some means of escape or communication with the outside world. The bright, airy house was decorated in white. White, sheer curtains from ceiling to floor danced gently in the breeze. The smell of the surf mingled with the aroma of merry flowers tickling the windowsills and peering into the house from the garden. "This is the living room," said Errol. "There are tropical fish over there in the pond."

To Stephen's astonishment, there was a pond filled with tropical fish in the center of the living room. A white, circular sofa surrounded the pond. "This room is quite tranquil," said Errol. "You can sit here for hours watching the fish and smelling the flowers. I spend many hours here. I hope that we can be friends, Stephen."

"I have friends, Errol," said Stephen caustically, "and I would like to join them." Errol's expression caused Stephen to soften his tone. "I'm sorry to be disagreeable, Errol, but you must understand my position."

"Your disposition will improve after a few days here. This is the library," said Errol. The floor to ceiling bookshelves impressed Stephen.

"I didn't know that Southgate cared about books," said Stephen.

"There are many things you can learn about Sheridon, Stephen. He's really not a bad sort. He reads incessantly and knows about everything. Sheridon spends most of his time in the library when he is here." Stephen surveyed the books on the shelf. There was an eclectic assortment of books on every topic imaginable.

"How often does Southgate come here?" asked Stephen. Errol did not respond.

"I'd like to remain in the library awhile, if I may," said Stephen.

"You want to stay in the library?" asked Errol. "Why? I haven't even shown you the fitness area yet."

"My appearance will attest to the fact that I don't work out much," said Stephen. "The library will be fine."

"Whatever you say," said Errol. "I'll check on you in an hour or so, just in case you get bored with all of these books."

Stephen observed *The New York Times* on the table. "Is the paper current?" asked Stephen.

"Oh, yes," said Errol. "It's delivered every day," said Errol.

It was the first ray of hope Stephen felt since awakening. If the paper was delivered daily, then there was a chance for contact with someone apart from Southgate's household staff.

"Who delivers the paper?" asked Stephen.

Errol smiled. "Sorry, Stephen, but you won't have an opportunity to leave or converse with anyone off of the island until Mr. Southgate sends the plane. I'll see you in an hour or so," said Errol taking his leave.

Stephen's heart felt elated. The island was close enough to civilization to receive a daily *New York Times*. How often did Sheridon Southgate visit the island? Stephen's heart filled with hope. Southgate would not win this time. Stephen sat at the circular wooden table in the center of the floor and inspected the neat piles of books on the table. They were all first editions of classical literature. It was difficult to imagine that Sheridon Southgate read anything that was not connected to business. Stephen's attention focused upon the large, magnificently patterned Oriental rug that covered the library floor. The room did not seem congruous with Sheridon Southgates' lifestyle. Thoughts of Sara engaged Stephen's thoughts. To what lengths would Southgate go to ensure that Sara's experimental pregnancy was not disrupted? The key players seemed certain that Stephen would not reveal his plight to anyone, but they were wrong. He didn't know how, but Stephen resolved to find a way to share his horrific experience with the world-at-large.

April appeared in the doorway. She had changed into a blue short set.

"You seem to appear from nowhere, quite often" said Stephen. "You asked if you could be of assistance. I have a request."

"Name it," said April perkily.

"You mentioned that I will not have Internet access— understandable, in view of the circumstances; surely, there can be no objection to my using it for research purposes. Perhaps if I understood the procedure Mr. Southgate desperately wants to develop through my offspring, I would be able to lend my support."

"Sheridon has many books on the topic." April proceeded to the bookshelves.

"This type of research changes daily," argued Stephen. "The information in those books is already outdated. No, I would like to read recent peer-reviewed articles on the research. Those can be found in various research libraries online."

"If the articles are online," countered April, "they may be out-dated and inaccurate as well. Even reputable research institutions can manipulate their data to obtain the results they need to gain approval. "

April's change of tone and academic stance surprised Stephen.

"Granted, but I don't seem to have any other options," lamented Stephen.

"Perhaps I can assist you," said April twisting her hair into the tight bun Stephen observed during their first meeting. "I am working on my Ph.D. in bioethics. I can arrange to have peer-reviewed articles delivered with the paper."

"I assume that the articles will be hand-picked by Sheridon Southgate and will explain the virtues of the procedure," said Stephen sardonically.

"Unfortunately, you were right in that there aren't many options available to you during your stay here, Stephen, but we will try to accommodate you in any way that doesn't compromise the project."

"It is more than a project, April. A human life hangs in the balance, and countless other lives will be altered. Please, help me, April," pleaded Stephen. "Don't allow this atrocity to occur. You say that you are studying bioethics—this is not ethical."

"The procedure is open to many interpretations. The possibilities for research are infinite," asserted April.

"It is a human life—not research!" yelled Stephen.

"Same difference," said April calmly. "Dinner will be served at six. Our chef is the best on the continent and is quite insistent that dinner be served on time. We dress for dinner. You will find suitable attire in your room. Try to enjoy your stay, Stephen. Everything will be fine."

April resumed her playful posture and bounced out of the room. Stephen sat at the table in utter dismay. Freemont nestled near Stephen's bare feet. The coolness of the canine's nose on his toes brought immeasurable comfort.

•   •   •

A pristine, white linen table cloth graced the long, elegant dining room table, and a crystal candelabra bedecked the table. Champagne flutes adorned each place setting, and soft, white linen napkins provided a sublime elegance beneath the silverware. Stephen sat uncomfortably in his white dinner jacket. He was not hungry, but he did not want to spend any more time in his room. The room was to his liking, but he did not want to allow himself to become comfortable within his surroundings.

"The jacket is a perfect fit," said Errol sipping champagne. "Great job, April."

"I feel like a test specimen," said Stephen lifting his champagne flute.

"Quite the contrary," said Errol. "You are a great guest. Some of the characters we get around here are real…"

"Errol," admonished April, "I don't think that we should discuss the other visitors."

"Please do," said Stephen. "I am very interested."

"No," said Errol, "April is right. Say, where are my allergy pills? I'm supposed to take them at seven. That dog gets into everything. There isn't one place in the house where he hasn't been." Errol felt his pockets frantically. He stood up and surveyed the room.

"Where were you last?" asked April.

"I'll check the gym," said Errol. "I don't know why we had to bring that dog."

Errol hurried from the table in the direction of the gym.

"Problem?" asked Stephen sipping his champagne?

"Errol is allergic to dogs," said April. "But I suppose you discovered that when you took his allergy pills."

"I don't know what you're talking about," said Stephen smugly.

"If you have them, please return them," entreated April. "If Errol gets sick, we will have to return to New York." April searched Stephen's face. "Do you have the pills?"

"Of course not," said Stephen. "Aren't there pharmacies around here? How far from civilization are we? Why can't you phone and have more pills delivered."

"Errol breaks out in hives, and his throat swells without those pills," warned April. "If you have them, please relinquish them. Errol may become seriously ill."

"If I had the pills, I would relinquish them for my safe return home. I can assure you that Freemont has romped all over the house, especially within Errol's room. Freemont is quite thorough. Even the clothes Errol is wearing has a trace of Freemont. "

"That was a heinous thing to do," retorted April.

"No more heinous than keeping me here against my will," said Stephen. "I want to leave immediately."

"That is impossible. We have no control over the plane's arrival, so you see, Errol must have his medication. Please return it, or else he will suffer," implored April.

"I, too, am suffering. Have you not noticed?" asked Stephen.

April sighed. "All right, we can compromise. Internet access for the pills, but you mustn't let anyone know that I provided it."

"I want to return home!" demanded Stephen.

"We're as powerless as you. Don't you understand? Do you think that we like doing this?" April began to weep. "Please, Stephen, if Sheridon finds out, he will destroy Errol. There won't be a position available for him anywhere in the world. Sheridon has formidable connections. Please, help us."

Stephen considered her plea. "So then you and Errol are a couple?"

"Errol is my husband," said April. "This position is everything to him. He wants his own health club; Sheridon promised to establish him at the end of the year. He can't do it on his own."

"I suppose Southgate is financing your doctoral degree as well," reasoned Stephen.

"In a few months, I will complete my dissertation, and then I can take care of Errol. We won't need Sheridon. Please help us. Please give me Errol's pills," whimpered April. "I'll do anything you want, or if you'd rather, Errol will come to your room this evening."

"You and Errol are willing to offer yourselves to Sheridon's guests for a crummy health club and financial backing for your degree?" Stephen stood up. "I can't stay in the same room with you." Stephen threw Errol's medication on the table. "Here, take it. Come on, Freemont. Let's get some fresh air." Stephen left the dining room as April hastened to find Errol. The thought of April and Errol repulsed him. Southgate and his fiends had to be stopped. Stephen resolved to find a way.

•

After a long walk on the beach with Freemont, Stephen returned to his room to find a laptop computer with Internet access on his desk. Stephen's first thought was to email his friends and alert them of his plight, but he reasoned that Sheridon Southgate would find some other way to accomplish his maleficent plan and move Sara to an undisclosed location, where he would not be able to find her. He needed time to think. Freemont climbed onto Stephen's lap as he surfed the Internet catching up on the latest news. A small item caught his attention. It became apparent why Sheridon wanted him out of the way. A stem cell research conference was to be held in New York in early September. Stephen reasoned that voices of affirmation would cite all of the medical possibilities. People waiting for miracle cures would, surely, make their voices heard. But where were the voices of the discarded embryos? Where were the voices of the children, walking replacement cells for those in need? Stephen would be their voice. Through him, their grievous lives would be exposed. How would he leave the island in order to attend the conference? There was only one way. Stephen drafted an email to Jonathan. He read it several times before pressing the send button. It was the only way. Jonathan would get what he wanted; he always did. Stephen looked out of the window and felt the cool evening air caress his face. The sky seemed a pink and lavender swirl that cushioned brilliant, twinkling stars. Stephen inhaled the fresh, cleansing scent of the ocean air. The irony was that such an idyllic environment brought about a sense of unbridled freedom, but freedom was relative. Stephen's skin crawled as he felt the rough skin of the eagle's talons clutch his ankles and wrap its indomitable wing across his body once again. He braced himself to become Jonathan's *cupbearer* for the sake of his unborn child - a child without a future.

Chapter XXI

Stephen sighed deeply as he exited the taxi in front of the corporate apartments. Holding Freemont in his arms, he emerged tanned, rested, and surprisingly optimistic. The new doorman smiled broadly and opened the door.

"You're looking well, Mr. Lawrence. The vacation agrees with you and Freemont." The doorman rubbed Freemont's ears; Freemont licked his hand.

Stephen nodded and entered the lobby. He glimpsed his reflection in the mirror by the elevator. For some reason, his attention was diverted to the sparkling floors that shone effervescently in the reflection. Stephen placed Freemont on the floor and examined his reflection. His khaki shorts, green tee shirt, and flip flops gave the impression of a youthful man after an invigorating day at the beach, but he was far from that carefree youth. In point-of-fact, he had not been carefree for quite some time. His youth ended when he met Jonathan and Sara. At some point in time, Stephen assumed the life of privilege that was associated with those he loved. He was an insider, and he was becoming a power-player like the others. Moguls entrusted their futures to him, and he held their futures in his insecure, young hands. His hair seemed lighter from the sun, and his countenance seemed brighter. His overall appearance was one of health and vigor. For some reason, he was able to put the imminent eruptions on a back burner and focus on some new, idyllic presence that seemed to surround him. The elevator door opened, and Jonathan stepped out dressed in a crisp, gray suit and red stripped tie. He wore black shoes and carried a black briefcase. Stephen stared at him in amazement. Jonathan knelt down to pet Freemont.

"I saw your taxi arrive and thought that I would come down to meet you," said Jonathan calmly. Stephen remained silent as though he was viewing a complete stranger. Jonathan lifted Freemont from the floor and held him. "Oh, the suit — well, one must put forth a professional image for the students. I expect you will want to change into something more appropriate also."

Stephen continued to stare at Jonathan. It seemed that he was in some type of netherworld orbiting earth. Freemont nestled snuggly in Jonathan's secure arms. "I suppose you'll want to spend a few moments resting after your trip. I am certain that you are jetlagged after three days of air travel and endless connecting flights, but you will have ample time to rest after the brief meeting with the students. You *are* still planning to lend your support to this venture, are you not?" asked Jonathan.

"Yes," said Stephen. His voice sounded strange, almost as strange as Jonathan's newfound professional presence.

"Good," said Jonathan. "I know that you want to visit the Stem Cell Conference this morning also. I made breakfast, and I arranged to have a car transport you to the office."

"No, thank you," said Stephen warily. "I've had enough of your arranged transportation."

Jonathan smiled. "You're upset. I don't blame you, but we'll sort everything out after the meeting." He placed Freemont on the floor. "You don't mind if I take him with me, do you? Everyone missed him at the office."

"I don't mind," said Stephen.

"Everything will be fine, Stephen," said Jonathan. "Trust me."

Jonathan walked confidently out of the door with Freemont in tow and tipped the smiling doorman. It occurred to Stephen that the doorman alerted Jonathan when his taxi arrived. Yes, he would move out of the building and out of Jonathan's controlled environment. Stephen reassured himself as he stepped into the elevator that everything would change for the better. The Stem Cell Conference would signal the end of the Southgate tyranny. As the elevator ascended, Stephen's spirits soared.

* * *

The Twin Towers loomed majestically in the bright, morning sky. Stephen arrived at the security area in front of the elevators to find a new employee scanning identification cards through the security reader. It was the young guard's first day on the job, and he scrutinized each face entering the building. The job was a temporary one; he hoped to become one of New York's Finest someday. He appeared to be twenty-five or twenty-six years old. A reddish, elongated birthmark across the back of his right hand captured Stephen's attention. Stephen felt his back pocket for his identification card while trying not to stare at the peculiar mark on the young man's hand. He looked abashedly at the young monitor.

"I seem to have forgotten my wallet. I've been distracted lately. You'll let me through, won't you?" asked Stephen.

"I'm sorry, Sir, but I'm not allowed to let anyone up without scanning an identification card first," said the diligent young guard.

"Don't you have a list of employees? Check the list," urged Stephen.

"I wasn't given a list of employees, Sir. I was told that everyone had to have an identification card scanned. Would you mind stepping aside to let the others with ID go through?"

"Stephen looked around for someone to vouch for him. "This is ludicrous. I work here."

"Take the day off," laughed a man as the security reader accepted his ID card.

"Where is the head of security?" asked Stephen. "I'm in charge of a special function on the eighty-second floor, which will begin promptly at nine o'clock," insisted Stephen. "Please call the head of security."

"All right," said the young guard without ceasing to scan ID cards.

"What kind of day is this?" asked Stephen with annoyance as he moved to the side of the security area. After ten minutes lapsed, he approached the young guard again. Stephen spoke with exaggerated civility so as not to betray the agitation charging through his body. "Excuse me, but were you able to phone the head of security?"

"Yes, Sir," answered the young guard calmly.

"Well?" asked Stephen impatiently.

"He's on his way. He said that you'll need photo ID."

"Where am I supposed to get photo ID? I told you that I left my wallet at home," said Stephen with a shrill voice.

The young guard shrugged his shoulders.

"Never mind," said Stephen. "Look, when he comes, tell him I'll be outside by the fountain."

Stephen's urgent need for fresh air escalated, and he found himself in front of the festive sphere spouting crystalline water. He thought of calling the office, but he did not want Jonathan to know that he was so disturbed that he left his wallet and ID at home. He tried to maintain his composure, but he realized that he was really angry. The forgotten wallet was symptomatic of the anxiety coursing through his body. In a few hours, everything would be exposed, and his entire life would change. Everyone's life would change. He thought of Sara and the baby. What would become of them? Stephen tried not to think of them. Young children ran joyfully around the fountain. Every now and then, they would venture close to the sprinkling waters and try to place a hand or an arm into the soothing pool. Instantly, a uniformed guard appeared and ushered the children away from the jubilant waters.

The guards irked Stephen, who believed that such a beautiful area symbolized freedom — even for small children. The mirth-filled children were guided away from the waters. Surely rising at such an early hour to visit the Towers before the throngs of other tourists arrived should be worth a splash or two. Festive pink and white impatiens dangled atop the concrete seats and tickled Stephen's neck as he sat in the oppressive heat. Stephen tried to remember the last time that he felt happy. He admitted to himself that it was the brief, albeit calamitous moments he spent in Sara's embrace.

•　•　•

The festivities in the Summer Initiatives office on the eighty-second floor were off to a rather sluggish beginning until Nigel produced a box of Nikes in assorted styles and colors. The students shed their early morning grogginess as they stepped into their new Nikes, which were donated by the corporation. Ms. Earvin, quick to avert any signs of trouble, wisely took the last pair of Nikes, which both Lorenzo Gomez and Thomas Grant grasped at the same time.

"Come on, Ms. Earvin," pleaded Lorenzo. "Thomas's mother won't let him wear them to school, and he sure can't play basketball. What's he gonna do with 'em 'cept prance around fairyland?" Lorenzo swirled around like a ballerina; the students laughed heartily at his antics.

"That will be enough!" bellowed Ms. Earvin.

"Lorenzo can have the sneakers, Ms. Earvin," said Thomas graciously.

"Sneakers," muttered Lorenzo indignantly. "They're not sneakers. They're Nikes!" Lorenzo took the Nikes from Ms. Earvin and walked away shaking his head.

The atmosphere in Jonathan's office was tense. Daniel Cohen sat uncomfortably at his son's ornate desk, while Arnold Cohen paced furiously across the room. Jonathan sat in the plush, burgundy wing chair in the corner near his cello stand. He lifted Mitzi from the floor.

"Don't you dare play that instrument now!" ordered Arnold. Jonathan placed Mitzi in the corner.

"The students will wonder why we are in here," said Jonathan calmly. "Can't this be discussed after the celebration?"

"I want to know why Sheridon Southgate is here, and I want to know why you are here as well," said Arnold staring at Daniel.

"Stephen invited him, Grandfather," said Jonathan in a tranquil voice.

"Where is Lawrence? Why isn't he here? Where has he been all week?" demanded Arnold. He continued before anyone could respond. "Daniel, I want you and your buddy Southgate out of here."

"Sheridon wants to support his father's efforts," said Daniel.

"Don't be naive!" yelled Arnold. "He's up to something, and we will pay the price."

"Grandfather, you suspect everyone," said Jonathan. "Can't we be civil and simply enjoy the festivities without this havoc?"

Arnold confronted his grandson. "You think this is havoc? I'm telling you, the havoc has yet to begin. I want Southgate out of here!"

The door opened, and Sheridon Southgate entered.

"Your voices can be heard out there. What is going on? I heard my name mentioned."

"Get out of here, Southgate!" ordered Arnold.

Sheridon smiled. "I have news that will make you regret those words."

"Well, let's have it," said Arnold.

"I came here on this festive occasion to inform you that as we speak, your brother, Zachery, is being transported to a safe haven – a tropical paradise that will prohibit any intrusion from the military police. He will be safe and sound, and you needn't worry about him any longer. You may visit him whenever you like."

"What's he talking about, Dad? What does he mean? Uncle Zach died in Vietnam. What's he saying, Dad?" asked Daniel in a state of bewilderment.

"Get out of here, Southgate," said Arnold menacingly.

"Dad, what's he talking about?" persisted Daniel. Someone banged on the door. Simmons entered before anyone could respond.

"Arnold, you need to get out here. The security guards are arresting one of the students."

Arnold pounded the desk with his fist. Everyone exited the room. Two security guards held one of the students with his hands behind his back.

"What's going on here?" demanded Arnold.

"I'll tell you what's going on," answered one of the guards. "This one tripped me to keep me from going into that office. I'm taking him downstairs." The guard held Lorenzo's arms tightly behind his back.

"I'll be responsible for him," announced Arnold. "He's part of a special program that we're having here today. I would really appreciate it if you would allow him to remain."

"Sorry, but this wise guy's coming with me. Let's see how funny you are downstairs." The security guard led Lorenzo out of the door. Sheridon approached the remaining guard and led him into an empty office.

"I would like that young man released," said Sheridon calmly. "You know how playful kids can get. I'm certain that he meant no harm. It was a prank that got out of hand."

"You'll have to speak with Hobson," said the guard. "It's his call."

"Make it your call," said Sheridon placing five crisp one hundred dollar bills on the desk.

"Keep your money, mister," said the guard with disgust. "We don't work that way around here." The guard left the office to find more disturbances in the outer offices. The students were cheering fervently.

"He got away," said Simmons. "They think that he's in one of the offices or restrooms on the upper levels. The guard phoned for the police. The kid took his gun."

Arnold banged his fist on a desk and muttered something unintelligible. Winston hung his head and closed his eyes. Ms. Earvin's body began to tremble. Early retirement was beginning to look better every day.

Chapter XXII

Paraplegic, Zachary Cohen, clad in full dress uniform, assumed an erect position in his wheelchair. His friend, Brian, who had been helping him to remain in hiding, accompanied him for support and walked beside the wheelchair into the North Tower. Brian placed his hand on Zach's shoulder as they waited for the express elevator. The two friends produced identification cards that were provided by Sheridon Southgate, and they took the elevator to the forty-fourth floor and exited. On the forty-fourth floor, they entered a local elevator to the higher floors. It pleased Zach to know that Sheridon's plans were about to be derailed. No one should be able to wield such power. Sheridon's altruistic plan to whisk Zach, a deserter from the Marine Corps and presumed dead, to a safe location was really a guise to gain control over Arnold Cohen's corporation. The officer and gentleman would turn himself over to the military police to face charges of desertion after a brief visit with his brother, Arnold, who had not seen him since he left home to join the Marine Corps.

Zach, stunningly attractive with piercing, cobalt eyes, was only twenty-one and fresh out of college when he made his fateful decision to join the Corps. He was an officer, and he enjoyed every moment of his military life. Then came war, and it proved too much for him, so he fled, leaving behind the men under his command, many of whom perished on the battlefield of Vietnam. He never understood why the survivors never reported that he deserted them. They led everyone to believe that he was a fallen hero, and the Cohen family received his Purple Heart. To add to his shame, he sustained his debilitating injuries while in hiding. The land mine was a wedding gift that he had not anticipated, particularly on his wedding day to a Vietnamese peasant girl, who cared for him until she died of cholera. That was the past. He would set the record straight. No longer would he flee in shame.

As Zach and Brian entered the elevator, a tall, regal-looking girl with thick, wavy black hair caressing her shoulders stood behind the wheelchair of a dispirited woman with a graying bun pinned severely towards the back of her head. Zach nodded to the woman as he positioned his wheelchair beside hers. The young boy holding the side of the wheelchair was in the midst of an informative briefing and revealed to everyone in the elevator that he and his father were dressed identically. Guy Brielle, dressed in a blue-stripped polo shirt, khaki shorts, and sandals, was unusually gregarious.

"Look, Kate, that man's wheelchair has a motor," observed Guy.

Zach smiled at the youth. "It helps me to get around a lot faster," informed the veteran.

"Wow! That's a great uniform," remarked Guy. "What happened to your legs?"

"Guy!" shrieked Courtney standing beside him. "That will be enough." She looked at the marine to offer an apology. He averted his eyes quickly, but not before the stylish fashion maven observed his piercing, cobalt eyes. Suddenly, the eyes resonated with the voice, which was hauntingly familiar.

"You must factor the fractions," instructed the tutor patiently.

"I wonder if he has a girlfriend," thought the adolescent Courtney as she gazed into her tutor's piercing, cobalt eyes.

"Courtney," reprimanded Zach, "please focus your attention on this equation. If you fail your algebra test, I'll be fired from the tutoring program."

"Sorry," said Courtney looking at the equation. "Zach, why do you need this job anyway? Your family has lots of money. You live on the hill, and you go to that private school. My dad thinks that you and the other boys from that school are only tutoring in this program so that you can put it on your college applications to Yale and Harvard."

"What do *you* think?" asked Zach continuing to examine the equations.

Courtney considered for a few moments. "Well, you explain the problems a lot better than my teacher, and I'm learning how to solve these equations."

"Does it matter, then, if I use this tutoring experience on my college applications?" asked the stunningly attractive tutor.

"I guess not. What's your favorite color, Zach?" asked Courtney.

"I thought that you were going to focus on the equation," said Zach patiently.

"Why do you like algebra so much? You look at these numbers as if they were people. I'll bet you'd like me a lot better if I was a math wiz or something."

"I like you just as you are. You're Arnold's best friend's little sister," said Zach.

"I'm not little!" corrected Courtney indignantly. "I'll be thirteen next week—a teenager like you!"

"Lower your voice before they ask us to leave the library," whispered Zach. "If you're going to become a teenager like me, then you will need to master these equations. Now, let me see you solve this one." Zach wrote an equation on Courtney's paper. "If you solve this one correctly, I'll take you for an ice cream sundae."

Courtney scooped up her pencil and began to fill the paper with various calculations until she solved the equation successfully. True to his word, Zach drove her to Baumgart's ice cream parlor in his sparkling navy blue convertible. After enjoying her ice cream sundae with Zach, Courney felt like a queen as they pulled up in front of her crumbling brick house on the far side of town. Her friends, Rachel and Maggie, were jumping double-dutch on the sidewalk. They stopped, seemingly in mid-air, and watched in amazement as Zach parked in front of her house, opened the car door for her, and escorted her to the front porch. Courtney tried not to giggle.

"Get an "A" on the test tomorrow," encouraged Zach.

Courtney was all smiles as she watched him drive away. Her friends raced to the porch to share the momentous event.

"I'm going to get an *A* tomorrow on Mrs. Kershaw's test. I want Zach to be proud of me," said Courtney.

"First thing tomorrow, I'm joining that tutoring program," proclaimed Maggie.

"Zach bought me an ice cream sundae with everything on it," said Courtney smugly. "He even introduced me to his friends."

"Just think," said Rachel with excitement, "if you get an *A* on the algebra test tomorrow, he may take you for, oh my goodness...pizza!"

The girls' squeals of delight could be heard down the block.

"When I become a rich and famous model, Zach and I will spend the rest of our lives together," announced Courtney.

"Forever and always," said Maggie dreamily.

•   •   •

Stephen closed his eyes as he basked in the morning sun. His head rested on the colorful impatiens as they dangled onto the back of the seating area around the tranquil fountain. A brusque voice disturbed the restful environs.

"You the guy that needs ID?" asked a brawny man in a short-sleeved white shirt. Before Stephen could answer, the roar of an engine was heard overhead.

"That plane's awfully low," said the guard anxiously. All eyes watched the plane advance closer and closer to the North Tower. "Move out!" yelled the guard. "It's gonna hit!"

Parents grabbed their frolicking children near the fountain and ran towards the stairs leading away from the plaza and down to the street. They were joined by scores of others running in fear. Far too many remained in their places with anchors around their feet. Their eyes were transfixed. Stephen's mouth hung open in amazement as the plane rammed into the stalwart edifice. The smell of jet fuel and the clutter of flying debris encircled the area quickly. Tons of sheets of paper tinged with fire floated through the air, while scalding chunks of metal and bodies falling helplessly from the windows hit the ground with tremendous impact. Stephen, unable to move, felt a hand pulling him out of harm's way. He could not speak, see, or think. All was a blur. Stephen's legs felt suspended in the air as they were moving. He felt as though he was in a dream, and the surreal environment would disappear, if he could only awaken.

"Hurry!" said the jittery voice belonging to the hands guiding him. Stephen noticed blood on the sleeves of his crisp, white shirt. His head was soaked. Was it perspiration or blood? He placed his hand upon his forehead, but before he could retrieve it, all went black. The unknown hands carried the scarlet young man past hundreds of firefighters hastening towards the mutilated building and placed him on the ground beside other crimson bodies waiting to be placed into ambulances. The stranger disappeared into the throngs of anguished spectators. As Stephen was placed upon a stretcher and into an ambulance, wails and shrieks could be heard from the crowd. A second plane exploded and disintegrated as it collided with the South Tower.

Total darkness ensued as Courtney glimpsed the averted, piercing cobalt eyes and heard the sonorous voice one last time. The elevator walls shook with numbing force before the tomb of death descended with a thunderous clamor, banging against the walls with a staccato-like tempo. The horrific sound of the elevator's descent grew distant and indistinct on its way to destruction.

Chapter XXIII

A breeze filled with dust and debris greeted Lorenzo as he emerged from his hiding place in the men's room on the forty-third floor. He quickly lifted the bottom of his shirt and covered his nose. The smell of gas permeated the air. Looking around, his suspicions were confirmed. An earthquake must have occurred. He knew from health class that when an earthquake strikes, people should drop to the floor and take cover. For the past ten minutes, the youth had remained stretched out on the floor of the men's room waiting for the earthquake to subside. Though the building seemed to sway slightly, Lorenzo thought that the worse was over and that it was safe to once again run down the stairwell in order to elude capture. Something was amiss. Why would an earthquake produce so much gas? Why was the floor so quiet? Where were the other people?

Lorenzo walked around a disheveled office with desks strewn with papers. He should check on his mother and sisters. Without him, they would panic in an earthquake. The smell of gas made him nauseous as he pressed the numbers of his cell phone. His sister answered and summoned his mother with elation.

"He's alive! He's alive!" squealed his sister with delight. "He's on the phone!"

Lorenzo heard his mother's voice. "Thank God! You got out of there."

"Is everybody all right?" asked Lorenzo anxiously. "Did the earthquake do much damage?"

"Earthquake? Don't you know what's going on?" asked his mother. "Where are you? You're not still in the building, are you?"

"Yeah, I'm in one of the offices. What do you mean it wasn't an earthquake? What's happening?"

"Get out of there! The building is on fire, Lorenzo!" yelled Mrs. Gomez. "A plane flew into it; it's on all the stations. You get out of there. Get off the phone and get out of there!"

"Stop worrying, Ma, I'm fine. I'll just go down the stairs, that's all. Stop worrying, I'm all right. I'll see you later." Lorenzo placed his cell phone into his pocket and looked around for the nearest exit. When he opened the stairwell door, he was amazed. The wet stairs were to be expected. The smoke had activated the sprinkler system, but he was unprepared for the endless line of people descending the stairs silently on the right-hand side of the stairwell. Some were carrying others who had been injured or had become incapacitated. Silently, they marched looking straight ahead. A man of average build supported an injured man of enormous proportions. They stopped to allow Lorenzo to take his place in the line. Lorenzo stepped into the line and proceeded downward. The silence was disconcerting. The people were marching like school children. Ascending the stairs on the left were firefighters lugging seventy-five to one hundred pounds of equipment as perspiration dripped from their faces. Applause rang out as they climbed the stairs. Lorenzo had seen his share of firefighters putting out some of the fires he had started in acts of vengeance against enemies, but never before had he seen firefighters actually do what they had been trained to do—risk their lives to save others. Lorenzo wondered what kind of people would walk into a burning building when others were trying to escape? The answer presented itself immediately.

"Burn victim coming down!" yelled a voice.

A firefighter led a badly-burned woman down the stairs. Her eyes looked straight ahead as though she was in shock. She moved like the living dead. Burned skin fell from her body as she was helped down the left-hand side of the stairwell. The sight made Lorenzo tremble. "Ms. Earvin?" He stood incredulously as his principal, who had been searching for him on the upper floors, was led down the stairs. "Ms. Earvin?" whispered Lorenzo.

"Don't look, Son," said a voice behind him. "Just keep moving."

Tears filled the youth's eyes as he kept the slow, deliberate pace of the line. Lorenzo took his shirt off and passed it down to the woman in front of him, who seemed to be choking on the dust in the air. Without looking back or speaking, she placed the shirt over her nose and proceeded downward in the hushed line. Without his shirt, Lorenzo had nothing to put before his nose to keep the dust out. His throat felt parched and clogged with dust; he felt that he might lose consciousness, but he continued to keep pace with the line. Miraculously, a small bottle of Poland Springs water was passed up to him. Was he dreaming? A quick glance down the line indicated that someone was passing bottled water up the line for each person to take a swig and then pass the bottle on to the next person in line. Lorenzo took a drink from the bottle, turned around, and held it to the mouth of the man behind him, who was now carrying his fallen colleague on his back. The line continued in surreal silence.

• • •

Papers and office equipment carpeted the conference room floor. The large mahogany table was reduced to an incline plane and resembled a children's sliding board as it stood on its two remaining wobbly legs. Arnold sat near the window cradling Daniel Cohen's bloody head on his lap. Daniel lay in a semi-comatose state. Arnold applied pressure to the gash on Daniel's forehead with the jacket of his suit. "What's taking so long?" asked Arnold impatiently. Nigel dialed 911 again on his cell phone.

"The line's still busy," said Nigel.

"Well, keep trying!" bellowed Arnold. "What are you doing, Southgate? Give that phone back to him."

"I must call Kate and tell her not to come down here," said Sheridon anxiously. "She'll be worried."

"No personal calls, Southgate," demanded Arnold. We don't know how long we'll be up here, and we can't risk running the battery down. Emergency calls only."

"My wife and son are on their way here! That is an emergency!" yelled Sheridon.

"Winston went to take care of that. I'm sure he had time to call them and alert them. Besides, this is probably all over the news by now. She'll know not to come," said Arnold.

Sheridon called Kate's cell phone number.

"Well?" asked Arnold.

"The phone is ringing, but there is no answer. I guess they're safe if the phone is ringing," reasoned Sheridon.

He returned the cell phone to Nigel, who was observing the door frame. "I think we'll be all right in here until they come for us," assured Nigel.

"Who's coming for us?" asked Darlene. "Who even knows we're in here?"

"We can't be the only people left on the floor," said Arnold. "There must be others out there. We will be rescued."

"I think that one of us should go for help," said Jonathan calmly. "I volunteer."

"No!" retorted Arnold. "It's too risky. There's too much smoke out there, and the walls may cave in. I'll go."

"Be realistic, Grandfather. I'm the most logical choice," reasoned Jonathan. "Your heart may not endure eighty-one flights. Besides, you need to care for Dad."

Arnold looked at his son and reflected upon years of Daniel's poor judgment. Of all days to return to the offices, Daniel selected this horrific day. Arnold shook his head.

"I got through!" yelled Nigel with excitement. He spoke loudly as though he feared the phone would not reproduce his voice. "Hello? We're on the eighty-second floor. Get us out of here!"

"Give me the phone," ordered Sheridon. "This is Sheridon Southgate. I'm in a conference room with five other people. The outer offices have severe damage, and the walls seem on the verge of collapse. We need advisement as to cleared exits. Which stairwells are passable? What do you mean you don't know? Aren't there emergency people in the building? What? The South Tower has been hit by a plane too? What do you mean too?" Sheridon turned to face the others. "A plane flew into this building and another one flew into the South Tower as well. That must have been the explosion we heard."

"We're under siege!" shouted Nigel.

"Quiet!" said Arnold impatiently. "What else are they saying, Southgate?"

Sheridon's voice quivered as he spoke into the cell phone. "All right. We'll wait here until help arrives. No, not Building Five—we're in the North Tower! We're in Suite…Hello? Hello!" Sheridon looked at the silver cell phone. "We were cut off." The group stared at one another in silence.

"Let's not panic," said Arnold calmly. "They'll get us out of here."

"No one knows where we are," said Jonathan. "I'm going to get help."

"He's right," said Sheridon. "Someone has to go and let them know that we're in here. The smoke is getting thicker, and Daniel needs immediate medical assistance. I would go, but I have bouts of asthma."

"I'll go with him," said Darlene. "I'm not afraid of the smoke. I been in lots of fires."

"I'll go too," said Thomas Grant, who had been standing silently gazing out of the window.

"You can't go," yelled Darlene. "You won't make it past the front room, and we'll have to spend our time rescuing you. Your momma ain't here to help you, Thomas."

"That's enough," said Arnold. "Thomas, you can remain here with me. Nigel, you go with them. There must be firemen on the stairwells," said Arnold hopefully. "Just take the stairs down until you find them. Tell them where we are, and tell them that your father has a serious head injury. Be careful."

Jonathan, Nigel, and Darlene opened the door and exited quickly. Sheridon closed the door to prevent additional smoke from seeping into the room.

"What are you looking for?" asked Arnold.

"Duct tape," said Sheridon. "If we seal the door, it will lessen the smoke entering the room."

"I think that you'll have to break a window to let the air in," said Arnold.

"You're right. I'll help you move Daniel away from the window," said Sheridon.

The two adversaries moved Daniel, who was bleeding profusely, to a corner away from the window. Sheridon used a metal paperweight and slammed it repeatedly against the cracked window. He took off his shirt and wrapped it around his cut, bleeding hand. As the air circulated around the room, Sheridon looked out of the window. The sight was overwhelming; he gasped.

"What is it?" asked Arnold applying more pressure to Daniel's head wound.

"People are jumping," said Sheridon slowly. "They're jumping out of the windows!" He turned away from the window and looked at Arnold with terror in his eyes.

"They'll send help!" reassured Arnold. "We can't panic. Help is on the way. They'll be here."

Sheridon's eyes turned towards the window again.

"Come away from that window, Thomas!" yelled Arnold. Thomas Grant stood frozen at the window.

Sheridon's vacuous expression and unsteady gait added to Arnold's sense of trepidation. "They'll be here," reassured Arnold. "They'll be here."

The two rivals sat helplessly as smoke seeped into the room with a vengeance.

• • •

"The exit is over here," announced Nigel through his shirt, which he held over his nose. His eyes teared from the wrathful smoke.

"One moment," said Jonathan hastening to the remains of his office.

"Where are you going?" asked Nigel.

""You two go ahead. I'll catch up." Jonathan climbed over the debris and entered his office. In the corner sat Mitzi, his cello, waiting patiently to be retrieved. Jonathan lifted the cumbersome instrument and climbed over the wreckage that was once the cheerful Summer Initiative offices.

"I can't believe you wasted time going to get that thing," said Darlene angrily. "Your father is bleeding to death, and you're trying to rescue that fiddle."

"It's a cello," corrected Jonathan mildly. "Where's Nigel?"

"He went to the stairway to look for help like he's got some sense. Come on, let's go."

"Wait," said Jonathan. "Did you hear something?"

"Hear what? I can't hear nothin'," said Darlene. "Come on, we gotta get outta here."

"Wait, there it is again," said Jonathan remaining still. He placed Mitzi on the wet floor gingerly and walked towards the clutter of dismantled desks.

"I'm goin'!" yelled Darlene.

Jonathan knelt down under one of the shattered desks. There, under a piece of metal, lay Freemont, motionless. The dog's eyes searched Jonathan's.

"Hey, boy, you got yourself into quite a bind." Jonathan stroked the dog's head. Freemont licked Jonathan's wrist weakly. "Don't worry. I'll get you out of there."

"I'll hold the desk up; you pull him out," said Darlene through a coughing spasm.

"Thanks. Freemont thanks you also," said Jonathan.

"Will you just come on?" yelled Darlene as she strained to lift the end of the collapsed desk. "This thing is heavy."

Jonathan lifted Freemont carefully. He held the dog close to his chest. "I think his legs are broken. I need something to wrap him in."

"Don't look at me. I'm already walking around in my bra." Darlene and Jonathan were using their shirts to shield their faces from the smoke. Jonathan surveyed the room. The bright blue and white felt banner heralding the commencement of the Computers-in-Schools Program was now sooty gray and soaking wet. "We can use that," said Jonathan nodding towards the banner. Darlene wrung the water out of the banner, folded it, and looped it under Jonathan's arm. She tied it at his shoulder and placed Freemont into the makeshift sling. "You're quite good at this," said Jonathan impressed with her tender way of handling Freemont.

"I'm gonna be a nurse," said Darlene matter-of-factly. "Come on, let's go."

"Wait!" yelled Jonathan. "What about Mitzi?"

"Mitzi? Who is Mitzi?" asked Darlene.

Jonathan tried to lift the cello lying on the wet floor, but he could not carry it without disturbing Freemont, resting peacefully against his chest. Darlene sighed and lifted the cello.

"Freemont and I are indebted to you," said Jonathan.

"Can we get out of here now?" asked Darlene coughing furiously.

• • •

Thomas Grant stood by the broken window looking out over the brilliant, sunlit city. He glanced towards Arnold, still holding his son's bloody head in his lap. Smoke and gas fumes filled the air.

"He's dead, isn't he?" asked Thomas resignedly.

Arnold looked blankly into space.

"Mr. Southgate's dead too," said Thomas. His gaze shifted towards Sheridon Southgate, who lay curled in a fetal position near the door. Gray, ashy smoke seeped through the door and caressed Sheridon's lifeless body.

"The rescue workers will find us, Thomas," said Arnold softly. "It's only a matter of minutes."

"You don't have to protect me from the truth, Mr. Cohen. I know they're dead; we'll be dead too," said Thomas.

"You mustn't talk that way, Thomas," said Arnold reassuringly.

"I'm not afraid to die, Mr. Cohen. I think about it all of the time. I wish for it sometimes."

Arnold looked at Thomas. "Why don't you come over here with me, son?"

"I wonder what it's like? They say you see a light, and everything is peaceful. Do you believe that, Mr. Cohen, that everything can be peaceful somewhere?" asked Thomas

Arnold sighed. "Yes, I do, but you must think of living, Thomas. You have your whole life ahead of you. You're young and talented. You have everything to live for, Thomas, and you will live. You will live," asserted Arnold.

Thomas considered for a moment then turned back to the broken window. "That's what I'm afraid of, Mr. Cohen." Thomas filled his lungs with the smoky air before forcing himself through the broken window and falling, head first, from the eighty-second floor. Arnold stared incredulously at the shattered window.

Chapter XXIV

Winston Brielle pushed forcefully against a large chard of plaster blocking the exit in the dark concourse. Water surrounded his ankles. He stopped to catch his breath.

"Are you all right in there?" yelled Winston through the plaster.

"Yes, there seems to be some type of obstruction blocking the entrance on this side as well," said a clear, calm voice. "I think my leg may be broken."

"Don't worry. I think that I can move this," said Winston. He used all of his strength to push against the plaster. It clung to its position stubbornly.

"I can't move it," said Winston. "I need help."

"Is there anyone around to help you?" asked the voice calmly.

"It's pretty dark, but I see a light at the other end of the concourse. I'll try to go over there and get some help. Will you be all right?" asked Winston.

"I suppose," answered the voice. "What is your name?"

"My name is Winston Churchill Brielle," answered Winston. For some reason, he felt compelled to say his entire name.

"That's a curious name," responded the voice pensively.

"My father was a history buff and a World War II veteran," said Winston. "What's your name?"

"Harold Gibson. I work on the thirty-fifth floor. Where do you work, Winston?"

"I'm with Cohen Enterprises on the eighty-second floor. I came down to wait for my sister, grandson, and daughter-in-law. I didn't see them anywhere around, so I think that they're safe. I'm afraid for my colleagues though."

"I'm sure that they made it out safely. Most of my co-workers were able to get out. I tried to exit through a shortcut near the Disney Store. I was near the exit when the ceiling collapsed."

"I will return with enough help to get you out of there, Harold. Hang on, all right?"

"Thank you, Winston."

Winston raced through the water covering the floor of the darkened concourse. The light at the other end was a hopeful sign. Muffled voices and the sound of shoes splashing through water could be heard in the distance. Winston's heart leapt with joy at the sight of the motionless escalator. People were descending with the help of a guard beaming a flashlight upon the stairs. Winston raised his arms and waved vigorously to attract the guard's attention. A sharp pain shot through his chest. Winston placed his hand to his chest; his face contorted as he sunk to the sodden floor. The guard noticed the descending image and heard the sound it made as it splashed into the water. He gave his flashlight to the next person disembarking from the escalator stairs and hurried towards the image.

"Where are you? Make some kind of sound!" yelled the guard. "Hello? Where are you?"

The guard looked around, but without a flashlight, he could not see the image. A cool, soft hand touched his, and he started. A petite woman with feathery brown ringlets seemed to appear miraculously. She stood smiling next to the guard.

"Where did you come from?" asked the guard as he scrutinized the woman's face. The mysterious personage seemed unscathed by the calamitous circumstances. "Did you see a man fall down over here? I saw a shadow lift a hand, and then I heard a splash in the water."

"Someone is trapped within an enclosed area near the exit. The person you saw was trying to direct you to him," said the woman.

The voice was melodic. The guard wished that he had his flashlight, but even without light, the woman's presence seemed to radiate a glow.

"You must hurry," said the woman with deliberation. "There isn't much time."

"Wait. I think I see the guy over there." The guard hastened towards the fallen image. Water surrounded Winston's body as it lay face down on the concourse floor. The guard turned Winston over onto his back and checked his pulse with his right hand, which bore a reddish, elongated birthmark. "His pulse is gone," said the guard softly. He placed Winston's hands across his chest. "Where did you say the other person was?" The guard looked up, but the woman was gone. "A real nutcase, she was," muttered the guard to himself. Winston's body cast a surreal glow around the immediate area. The faint smell of honeysuckle permeated the air. The guard scratched his head and moved slowly in the direction of the plaster entrapment. As he approached, a deafening explosion resounded before the battle weary edifice collapsed and disintegrated into its own white dust.

Chapter XXV

The Service of Remembrance commemorating the catastrophic events of 9/11 at the Cathedral of St. John the Divine was dark and silent, save for the flickering candelabras on the High Altar and the hushed voice reading the names of the dead. The voice was non-descript and expressed no emotion as the surnames beginning with the letter "A" were read. A man with bowed head emerged from the side of the Cathedral as if in a procession and coordinated his steps with the rhythm of each name read. He passed a young woman with a blonde ponytail, who stood off to the side of the steps leading to the High Altar holding a small recorder in the air to preserve an enduring memory of the name of her loved one. The infinite list of names was read by rotating speakers, all with the same hushed voice of solemnity.

Stephen Lawrence, accompanied by his family, approached the front of the Cathedral and sat in the wooden chairs near an area with black music stands and chairs in preparation for the memorial concert to be held later in the evening. A black grand piano and sound speakers blocked the view of the High Altar. The "A" names were completed. A brief interlude with sorrowful chamber music preceded the reading of the "B" surnames. Sara

Lawrence placed eight-month-old Jonathan Arnold Lawrence onto her husband's lap. The baby slept peacefully in his father's arms.

"Place this over him," said Elizabeth Cohen passing a small blanket to her son-in-law. Stephen covered his son and beheld him with wonderment. The angelic bundle of joy bore a striking resemblance to his deceased uncle, Jonathan. Susannah Cohen gazed lovingly at her great-grandson as a tear trickled down her cheek. As the viola cried and the violin mourned, Stephen became aware of the music. It was Jonathan's chamber music group. An empty chair with one white rose across the seat marked a void that would never be replaced. Stephen trembled slightly. Sara snuggled close to her husband and kissed his forehead near the long jagged scar protruding from his temple to the bridge of his nose. Stephen refused plastic surgery. The scar helped to assuage feelings of guilt and enabled him to feel a part of the suffering of those trapped within the flaming inferno.

The music ended, and the "B" names were read. Stephen noticed the glistening of a reddish *fireball* at the end of the row. The frisky tyke with effusive red tresses sat restlessly on the lap of an older gentleman dressed in a worn, gray woolen suit. The suit had seen its share of funerals, weddings, and other formal occasions. The gentleman's gray hair with sullen red strands evoked a bygone era of youth and vitality. A gray-haired woman in a blue-paisley flowered dress sat next to the pair. The effervescent youth leaned her head against the gentleman's chest as a new reader read the names. The flaming *fireball* jumped to the floor and ran to the other end of the row to see the strange little dog with two legs. His hind parts were attached to a contraption with two small wheels that enabled him to move around. She laughed and frolicked with Freemont. The gray-haired gentleman apologized and whisked the young lass up quickly. They returned to their seats.

The sun shone cheerfully outside of the Cathedral. Traffic flowed up Amsterdam Avenue without encumbrance. The young woman stood on the sidewalk and looked up at the Cathedral. The thought of attending the memorial service was overwhelming, and the thought of her classmates and mentors in the burning building was still raw within her mind. Darlene summoned her courage and began to climb the stairs. She walked quietly down the main aisle of the darkened Cathedral and approached the chamber music group, which was ending a sorrowful tune. Stoically, Darlene placed the broken, shattered Mitzi near the seat with the white rose. She turned around, looked straight ahead, and walked up the middle aisle to exit the Cathedral. Outside, she sat in the bright sunshine on the cool, cement Cathedral steps and, for the first time since the tragedy, wept inconsolably.

$$\bullet \quad \bullet \quad \bullet$$

The new reader had a female voice, and she read the names of the fallen with clarity and a sense of purpose. Suddenly, the young *fireball* sat upright and looked towards the High Altar. A smile of recognition appeared on her ruddy, cherub face.

"Courtney Anne Brielle...Guy Antoine Brielle...," said the reader solemnly.

The juvenile's face shone with radiant enthusiasm as she sat on Papa Sean's lap. Grandmother Maureen fidgeted in her seat nervously as her husband pinched his granddaughter's rosy cheeks.

"Winston Churchill Brielle...," continued the reader.

"Grandpa," whispered the crimson-haired lass excitedly. Papa Sean placed his granddaughter's head against his chest.

"We must tell her, Sean," said Grandmother Maureen softly. "She thinks that she's going to see them after the service. We must tell her."

"Quiet yourself," whispered Papa Sean. "No need to upset the little darling's heart. We'll tell her when we return to Dublin."

The woman's countenance fell. She closed her eyes and dropped her head in silent prayer. Papa Sean reconciled the death of his only daughter as an act of fate. Despite his persistent warnings, Kate married the interloper. Papa Sean knew that it would end in tragedy. At the conclusion of the service, the family would board the Aer Lingus flight with a stopover in Shannon, and return to Dublin. They would never return to the United States, and Taylor's brief acquaintance with her American relations would end with the reading of their names.

The chamber music began anew. Stephen felt a touch on his shoulder. He looked up into the eyes of a young man. He extended his hand. "Mr. Lawrence, I just wanted to thank you for everything you've done," said the young man.

Stephen smiled and shook Lorenzo Gomez's hand. "We're all proud of you," said Stephen.

"The recommendation you gave me really helped me get into college. I'm training to be a firefighter. I just want to thank you. If there's anything I can ever do for you..."

"As a matter of fact, Lorenzo, there *is* something you can do." Stephen looked towards a small assemblage in the back of the Cathedral.

Nigel motioned for the group to remain quiet as the chamber music ended.

"How long we got to sit here?" inquired a student. "They only on the "C's.""

"Show some respect," said Lorenzo softly but firmly as he approached the group. "Are they giving you a hard time, Nigel?"

"They're a tad restless, but everything is under control," said Nigel.

Lorenzo inspected the new recruits into the Cohen Youth Enterprises Program, in which Stephen Lawrence, CEO, along with his intern, Nigel, prepared at-risk students for college and the corporate world.

• • •

The Hudson River meandered lazily beneath the George Washington Bridge. From the New Jersey side, New York seemed to dazzle in the sunshine despite the painfully empty space at the lower end of Manhattan. High atop the spires, a lone eagle gazed intensely across the lush, emerald grounds of the high school. A few students chatted quietly near the pond. The eagle spread its massive wings, expended a deafening screech, and took flight into the crystal blue heavens.

The End